Gras

Debra Kayn

Grasping For Freedom
1st Digital release:
www.debrakayn.com

To my readers

Thank you to every one of you who made the writing of Torque's story one of the greatest experiences I've had so far publishing. The love and encouragement I received put extra excitement into this story for me. The emails from my readers became crazy and demanding, and left me smiling all day long. You all are an author's dream audience. Thank you for hopping on for the ride.

After each new release, I'm bombarded with emails and questions asking me which Bantorus member will have the next book. Now, I'm not going to give the surprise away yet, but you can rest assured, there will be more bikers. They demand more stories, because they're bossy…and too damn sexy to turn down. Besides, the bikers are as much a part of me as I am of them. Let's roll…

Dedication

Wheels
Because of you, these books are never-ending.
Thank you for giving me the happy.

CSC

It's a lifestyle. It's an attitude. It's badassery at its best.
I totally said that in the dedication for Soothing His Madness too, but without each one of you, there would be no moments, no memories, no experiences, so I could write these books. Between leathers, patches, fringe, motorcycles, grease, laughs, Fireballs, you all make my world go round.

Chapter One

The rough idle of Torque Kendler's Harley Davidson muffled the conversation between the two women outside Cabin D. Torque cut the engine, toed the stand, and moved off his motorcycle. Sometime between last night and this morning, the new gal— Brandy, had arrived in Pitnam to take over Gladys's position as the manager of the bar.

Gladys's shoulders rounded even more as she glanced over at the line of motorcycles lined up in the parking lot and shook her head, looking every bit her age today, before walking toward her vehicle with slow steps. Torque clenched his teeth and swallowed past the emotions of what Gladys's leaving meant.

At sixty-eight years old, Gladys deserved to retire and spend her free time enjoying her activities away from the bar. He exhaled loudly. She was every Bantorus member's surrogate momma and knew every secret, every story, and every bit of scandal that rocked Pitnam.

The MC members were obligated out of love and respect to let her enjoy the rest of her years without burdening her with club business. He'd continue to protect and look after her, because he'd personally promised her deceased husband, Willy, she'd remain part of the family for life. Gladys was Bantorus, through and through.

Gladys leaving left a hole within the club that a younger, more energetic woman at the headquarters of Bantorus MC would never be able to fill. He gazed back at Brandy. The chick wasn't what he expected. Rain, the president of the Bantorus Motorcycle Club, described her as smart, educated, and most of all reliable.

First impressions shot down each one of those qualities.

Her hair—long and blonde, but dyed black underneath nearly hit her waist. A slim waist above an ass used to bouncing on a man's dick. No way could a woman walk with loose hips and that much confidence without knowing exactly what she was doing to every man watching her. He leaned against the wall and refused to look away when Brandy's gaze hit on him outside the door.

High cheekbones, angled chin softened by full lips almost distracted him from the narrowed eyes. Green eyes stared intently at him, making him wonder how in the hell a woman like her found herself in Pitnam. Or, how Rain found her through his contacts.

Brandy's eyebrow lifted. The small silver round ring at the edge of her brow picked up the glare from the setting sun and seemed to taunt him. His breath caught in his chest. From outside appearances, she was any biker's fantasy with her tight jeans—ripped at the thighs, her chrome spikes on black leather boots tilting her tits and ass out to an angle he appreciated.

She fit right in with the bitches hanging around the bar.

Yet, she was different from any of the girls or old ladies at the club. Those differences rubbed him the wrong way. Independence, lack of respect, over confident, and opinionated were qualities in a woman he typically avoided.

Besides his irritation with the newly acquired manager, there were too many changes happening around him lately to trust anyone new. His shoulder throbbed reminding him of the dangers that had infiltrated his town lately. Bantorus Motorcycle Club was on tender ground and Pitnam wasn't the safe haven it was years ago.

Los Li, part of the Mexican mafia, shot him twice in the last ten months, and almost took the lives of two women belonging to Bantorus members. Men were dropping like flies for their old ladies and settling down. Now Gladys leaving Cactus Cove left him wanting to escape on a long ride to avoid the turmoil that came with changes.

For some reason, this new chick bothered him and he couldn't figure out why.

Brandy walked toward him with long strides, showing off her killer legs again. He remained where he was, not taking his gaze off her. She surprised him by staring back, all the way to the door. She continued her stare down as she grabbed the handle, twisted, and walked into the bar.

Finally, the door closed blocking her from his sight. He blew out his cheeks. Shit. She was a piece of work.

The door swung open again and Brandy stepped out of the building, crossed her arms, and said, "What the hell is your problem?"

A bitch with a mouth on her.

He lowered his gaze and took in the heaving breasts under her skintight T-shirt. He moistened his lips, surprised to find he wanted to keep her mouth busy so he didn't have to listen to her attitude.

"Ah, I see." She lowered her arms and pointed at her chest. "Take a good long look, buddy, because that's all you're going to get from me."

He tilted his head and spoke to her tits. "Is that so?"

He saw movement coming from his left and grabbed her wrist before her hand made contact with his face. "I'll only tell you this once, so listen closely. You ever try to hit me again, and I'll hit you back."

She covered her shock well, except for the swift intake of air. "You'd hit a woman?"

He never had before, but he didn't want her to test him. There was only so much he'd accept and taking shit from anyone, man or woman, wasn't going to happen. "All you need to know is I'm an asshole who you need to stay away from."

She dropped her gaze to the hand holding her arm. Underneath his fingers, her skin warmed and he allowed himself to soak in the heat.

He relaxed his hold and put her arm down at her side. "Stay away from me."

She stepped back, biting her lip. Without saying a word, she walked inside the bar, leaving him outside alone again. He rubbed his thumb against the palm of his hand, still heated from touching her. He cussed under his breath. Life around Cactus Cove was changing, and he could almost feel his calm slipping away.

Nothing fueled his anger more than another person attempting to control his freedom. Rain might've hired Brandy to run the bar, but she wasn't going to order him around. He walked toward his motorcycle. Gladys had known her place and knew when to keep the others away from him when he found society crushing in on him. He had a feeling Brandy was going to give him a push at the wrong time, and all hell was going to break lose.

The compressing pressure in his head intensified. His body ached deep inside where alcohol or escaping on his motorcycle couldn't touch. He shook his head trying to dispatch the thoughts narrowing in on him.

"Torque," Rain's voice came from behind him.

He stopped next to his Harley. The muscles in his face automatically relaxed to hide the chaos in his head. "Yeah?"

Rain's dark eyes studied him without speaking. Torque shoved his hands in his back pockets of his jeans. His president saw everything, but not all the time.

"I have to go up to Seattle. I'll be taking Tori and Lilly and making a day of it. She's got some shop or mall she wants to go to. Can you hang around here? Keep an eye on things?" Rain widened his stance and added. "Bruce is around, but it's Friday and I don't want Brandy to deal with everything by herself on her first day. The other members know she's off limits, but I'd feel better knowing someone had her back until she gets used to everyone."

He looked back at his bike, wanting to ride away and tell Rain no. "Yeah, I'll stick around."

Rain remained standing in front of him, his long hair loose and falling over his forehead. "Something going on?"

"No," he answered. "I'm good."

At least he would be when he could go home and get away from everyone. Over the years, he'd dodged more shit than he had bullets. Hell, he'd rather take another bullet than deal with a woman who closed in on him. He liked his privacy and space.

Rain clapped his hand on Torque's shoulder. "Pete, Remmy, and Slade are at the garage. Call them if you need a break. I'll give them the heads up to stick around."

"'Right," he said.

Rain walked to his motorcycle in sure, confident steps, and Torque headed back to the bar, each of his steps heavier than the last. Inside, he went straight to the pool table. He'd distract himself with a few games and time would fly, so he could go home. If that didn't work, he'd call in Slade. He trusted his MC brother and knew Slade wouldn't question why he needed to get away from everyone.

No one ever talked about his actions, his words, his threats, his spontaneous need to distance himself from everyone, including the club, in which he was glad. Talking never helped. He was who he was, and life consisted of him. Period.

Leaning over the pool table, he lined the cue ball and broke, watching the balls scatter across the green felted surface.

Two solid colored pool balls went in the side pockets, and he moved around the side of the table to take another shot. He often played pool by himself, wasting time, working out a problem, or while waiting for club business to be over.

Then again, he'd had years of practice entertaining himself. He was a solitary player, and preferred the quiet.

Raul approached and thumped the corner of the table with his knuckles. "Want to re-rack? I'm only wasting time while Crystal shows up."

"Nah, man, I'm good. Just watching the clock myself." Torque caught sight of Brandy behind Raul at the counter of the bar.

She leaned her elbows on the surface and displayed her ass for everyone to see. His gaze went down her legs, ogling the bare skin peeking through the rips on her jeans under the curve of her butt. She planted her feet farther apart. He shook his head and turned away. She was setting herself up for trouble.

"See you've met Brandy," Raul said, mumbling something in Spanish that anyone could translate as male appreciate for the opposite sex. "The old ladies are not going to like her once they get a look at her."

"Yeah, well, nobody can replace Gladys," he muttered.

Best thing that could happen was Rain's wife, Tori, or even Raul's old lady, Crystal, took Brandy aside and informed her how things worked within the club. Maybe the women could even force Rain to hire someone new…or someone older like Gladys. Hell, he'd even take a guy running the bar over Brandy, and he was never one to turn down an available woman.

"I agree, *amigo*. Gladys was the best thing for all of us." Raul's body shifted and he turned toward the door. "Looks like my woman came early."

Crystal stopped a few feet from the door and searched the bar. Her shoulders went back, displaying more of the cross tattoo on her chest that her low cut T-shirt couldn't cover. Torque could almost hear the hiss through Crystal's teeth as she curled her lip at the sight of Brandy. He planted the end of the pool stick between his boots and leaned forward to watch the show. For the first time today, the muscles around his mouth relaxed and he almost smiled.

Brandy had no idea the drama playing out behind her. Torque gazed back at Crystal. Raul's wife marched across the room with her arms swinging at her sides in a beeline toward the counter.

He'd seen what the Bantorus women would do to a bitch that got out of hand or didn't know her place. The female hangers were not allowed around the bikers during daylight hours, and definitely not when the old ladies were present.

He kept his gaze on the action. This was not going to end pretty and since he was in charge of looking after Brandy, he probably should do something.

"Eh, you might want to pull your woman in before there's bloodshed," Torque said.

Raul nodded and moved in a straight line. He intercepted Crystal with an arm around her waist and hauled her back before she was within arm's reach of Brandy. Torque watched him usher Crystal down the hallway, leaving Brandy unaware of the biker saving her ass.

Brandy spun around and caught him looking at her before he could bring himself to turn away. Challenged, he stared her down in case she believed she got the upper hand on him. He regretted his mistake the moment she planted her high-heeled boot in his direction.

He never had taken confrontations well. Seven years of hell early on in his life, he fought and protected his personal space. Old habits die hard, even on the outside.

"I see the vest. I see the flame tattoo on your neck. I see the badass attitude that makes you a Bantorus member. I also get how you have the freedom to come and go making your own rules, because you're part of the MC." She moistened her lips, and damned if his cock didn't hardened at the sight of her pink moist tongue. "But I will not have you interrupting my work day by pushing your authority in the bar or over me. You're not my boss, so get the hell out of here and find some other girl to entertain you."

"You going to make me?" he said, enjoying the banter too much for his liking.

Her gaze flickered and for the first time he noticed her hesitation. Then she stepped closer. "I'm serious. Don't fu—"

"Eh," he said, cutting her off. "Be careful, before I think of something else you can do with that dirty little mouth."

She scoffed and glared. "Get real."

He raised his hand, using his index finger to twine the strand of hair curling over the peak of her large breast pushing against her T-shirt. When he'd wrapped his whole finger, he tugged hard enough to catch her by surprise, causing her to stumble toward him. Her hands sprawled on his chest, and his body tensed in pleasure.

"I warned you. Stay away from *me*," he whispered.

Her breath quickened. "Or what?"

"You really want to know?" He stared at her mouth.

She paused with her lips parted. "Yeah. You talk big, but you're—"

He captured her mouth with his own, shutting her down.

Her full lips cushioned his. He gave her no warming, no softness, no chance to escape. He thrust his tongue into her mouth, stroking the velvety-softness in pure selfish lust. He swallowed her gasp, taking the opportunity to tilt his head to capture her bottom lip and go back for one more taste.

The tips of her nails scratched the sensitive scarred skin under his shirt. He growled, enjoying the pain. She made him feel past the pressure in his head. He sensed everything about her. Her strength, her softness, her taste—wild and hot, her smell—almost intoxicating and reminded him of honey and fresh air…freedom.

Brandy's hips tilted forward, pressing against his hardness. He groaned, leaning her back, taking her off balance so she had nowhere to go but to hold on to him. His breath escaped him and he closed his eyes, sucking, licking, demanding.

Then she was gone. He opened his eyes at the same time his hand jerked. She'd ripped her hair out of his grasp, and he curled his fingers, still holding a few stray strands that stayed with him.

She stared at him with wide, aroused eyes, an opened mouth, swollen and wet from his kiss. He glanced down at his hand and swallowed. He should never have touched her.

Chapter Two

Lightheaded and shocked from the kiss, Brandy stared at Torque. He was supposed to keep his distance. All men stayed away when she pushed them.

Not him, he took what he wanted and left her…confused.

"You asshole," she whispered, fingering her bottom lip where the skin still throbbed from the most possessive kiss she'd ever received.

Torque leaned closer. "I already gave you that information about me. Maybe you'll believe me now. I'm not playing your game. Stay the fuck away from me."

She retreated and walked toward the bar, unable to stand the heat coming off him. Everything inside of her wanted to retaliate and tell him what she thought of him putting her down…degrading her, embarrassing her. She wanted to scream. Instead, she kept walking.

She wanted to escape the bar, escape Bantorus MC, escape Torque, and not look back. She'd had a lifetime of attitude, and what had that left her? Absolutely nothing.

Bruce glanced at her while he wiped the counter down. "Everything okay?"

"Yeah." She nodded, convincing herself it was true.

She was an adult, holding down a managerial position, and surviving on her own. Other people's actions weren't a reflection on her. She was not responsible for what they did.

Her body flushed hot, not heated, not warmed, but one giant hot flash and she was only twenty-four years old. She glanced back at the man who instantly had her panting with this badass attitude. She couldn't explain why she reacted so badly toward him. Yet looking at him, he was the most beautiful man she'd ever seen, and the worst kind of man for her. She didn't need another hotheaded man in her life.

Torque represented bad news. All tough and dominating, even his looks pegged him as trouble. Longish brown hair swept back rather than brushed. Two days growth of whiskers as if he couldn't bother to shave. She inhaled swiftly, attempting to get control of herself. Broad shoulders, which his leather vest accented, added strength to his no-touch attitude.

But he'd touched her, and she'd liked it. She needed to figure out a way to hate him.

She'd spent years learning how to stand up for herself, to protect her weaknesses, and to live independently. None of her reactions to him made any sense.

"You know, Gladys worked here a lot of years. She ran the bar before Rain bought the business for Bantorus headquarters." Bruce set down a shot glass on the bar. "She was the first person I met when I was delegated to pouring drinks."

"Is that so?" she mumbled, watching him pour whiskey into the glass.

"Yep." Bruce slid the glass over in front of Brandy. "I'm also the one who knew that she got through the day by tossing back a whiskey now and then. Drink up, sweetheart. You need the calm."

"I can't." She eyed the glass, really wanting to wash away all the feelings of turmoil circling her stomach.

"Go on…" Bruce put the glass in her hand. "If only to wash the taste of Torque out of your mouth."

She lifted her gaze and met Bruce's wink. Amusement danced in his eyes, but he thankfully didn't say another work about what happened with Torque. She tipped back the drink and swallowed in one large gulp to hide from the truth. Her chest exploded in a blazing ball of fire. She breathed out and sucked in air, which made her cough.

She accepted the glass of Cola Bruce handed her, and drank half of the liquid before she was able to find her voice. "Thanks."

"No problem." Bruce winked. "You best go talk with the waitresses and prepare them for the evening crowd. Once this place picks up, you won't have another chance to organize the team."

"Right." She smoothed her shirt over her trembling stomach.

Taylor, the petite waitress with adorable brown hair and a scar across her cheek had shown her the back room and where to locate all the supplies during her orientation earlier, stood waiting for instructions with raised brows. Ginger, the outspoken red haired woman who assessed her up and down and forced a fake smile when Rain introduced her, looked everywhere else but at

Brandy. They were polite, but standoffish. She'd expected their attitude, because she was new, she was female, and they'd just finished a going away party for a dear friend and boss.

While she went over rotations, break schedules, and the procedures on what the waitresses should do if they ran into trouble, Brandy kept her back toward the pool table and Torque. The whiskey helped calm her, and by the time she checked in on the cook, took inventory for Bruce, and stocked under the counter, she felt more like herself.

The evening crowd showed up and settled in at the bar and tables. A cluster of bikers congregated around the pool table, making a sea of leather vests, and making it more difficult to keep watching Torque—which she wasn't going to do.

Work wise, things were improving for her first day on the job.

Her cell phone vibrated in her pocket. She searched for Bruce and found him talking to an older biker sitting at the bar. Ginger sat on a man's lap in the corner, and the way she gyrated, she wasn't paying any attention to anyone else. She gazed at the pool table and found Taylor leaning into Slade, whom she'd met earlier and knew was Taylor's man. With everyone's eyes off her, she hurried down the hallway and out the back door. Only then did she remove her phone from her pocket.

Knowing she missed the call and the blackened out screen would give her no information on who called, she waited. The instructions from her boss were strict. If she didn't pick up, she'd receive another call in exactly three minutes. If she missed the connection a second time, she'd be removed from the area with no warning. Her life depended on her answering the phone.

Her phone vibrated. She pushed the side button. "Hello?"

"In three more days, we'll contact you. At that time, we need an idea on the number of Bantorus members and any information about their schedule," said the voice on the other end of the call.

Hired by Los Li after she turned to the wrong person for help, there was only one thing she could do until she found a way to get her father out of danger. She had to go along with her job of gathering information about Bantorus MC before her dad got himself killed.

She recognized the caller as the man she knew as Radiant. Nothing about him cast a glow around him like his name suggested. She suspected he was one of the main leaders within Los Li, and he got his name because he was the brains behind everything they did. Not that she knew what their business was, but the secrets and people who came and went within their headquarters were bad, real bad.

"Okay." She nodded, though she knew no one could see her. "You'll need to give me time, because only Rain—who isn't much of a talker, and the bartender here is reaching out to me. Most of them…they don't like outsiders, so they're not sharing anything I can't see myself."

"I'd suggest you change their minds then, baby," said Radiant.

She thrust her fingers in her hair. His suggestion was the obvious one, but the last thing she wanted to do was lower herself to whoring herself out. That was the main reason why she came to Pitnam. It kept her away from sleeping with the members of Los Li in exchange for her dad's life.

"I'll think of something," she said.

Silence greeted her. She looked at the display—still black, and put the cell back on her ear. "Hello?"

No response. She pushed the button on the side of the phone again and shoved the device in her pocket. Already she felt like a failure.

She opened the door and walked back inside Cactus Cove. She had no idea why Los Li wanted information on Bantorus MC, and she didn't care. She had to find her dad before she lost him too. She was too young and blind to what her mother had gone through, but she could stop her dad from self-destructing.

No matter what anyone else said—friends, coworkers, her dad's old buddies—she was the only person who could help her dad, the only one who could make him listen. Now that her mom couldn't keep David Haas on the straight, she was responsible for him.

The arid and yeasty smell of beer hit her in the hallway. She paused on the outskirt of the room, gathering herself. She only had a few more hours and then she could go out to the cabin.

A large man with a black skullcap walked toward her. She smiled and looked away to discourage any conversation. The man kept coming. She stepped to the side and his beefy hand circled her waist and brought her up flat against his chest.

"Excuse me," she said, pushing on his arms.

"That's it, honey." He tugged her closer, breathing on her face. "I like a bitch with fire."

"I said, excuse me." She shoved, but all she did was exhaust her strength. "Let me go, you—"

The man whirled around, losing his hold on her. Brandy stumbled, gaining her balance and heard a sickening pop followed by a thud. She jerked her gaze toward the man, who now lay flat on his back on the floor.

Torque stood above him, rubbing his hand. "She ain't one of the bitches, Graham."

Graham pushed up on his elbows. He glanced between her and Torque. "Sure looks like a bitch to me."

Torque planted his boot in the middle of Graham's chest and pushed him back down. "Apologize. Now. She's the new manager."

"Ah, hell," Graham muttered. "Sorry, honey. I didn't know you were working for Rain."

Uh. Well. Wow. She pulled her gaze from Torque and glanced at Graham. "It's okay."

She turned to tell Torque thank you, but one look from him and she knew it would be better to walk away. She ducked her chin and turned around. Hiding out in the kitchen wasn't her plan, but that's what she did. She took the time to make small talk with the cook, help hand out ketchup bottles to Taylor, and finally joined Bruce behind the bar when her heartbeat settled into a familiar pattern.

The counter provided a shield between her and Torque, and meant she could relax. She poured a few mugs of beer and chatted with a couple named Pauline—who ran Pitnam's newspaper and was the old lady to Orca—who was huge. Before she knew it, Bruce announced last call. She glanced at the clock behind the bar. Ten more minutes and the bar closed.

"Are they really going to have time to squeeze in another drink?" She studied the crowd.

Bruce laughed. "You must not spend a lot of time around bikers."

"No, not really," she said.

At least ten guys lined the bar. Each one grabbed a mug and without stopping, downed the whole drink. She almost laughed at the hooting and hollering that went up from each one after they finished. Fascinated, she watched each one of the men throw their arm over the closest woman and head for the door.

She whistled softly and grinned at Bruce. "That puts a whole new meaning to hooking up at the bar, huh?"

"You'll see a lot of that here, but only when Tori's not around. She doesn't put up with the girls hanging around the bar anymore." Bruce slid his fingers through the handles of the mugs and deposited them in the plastic bin behind the counter. "Most of those women are bitches, and—"

"Excuse me?" She raised her brows. "Not very professional of you to call them a derogatory name. They're customers."

Bruce grinned. "Nah, they're bitches. A few of them live in the biggest cabin in the back…three doors down from the cabin you claimed. They're here for the Bantorus men. We've got old ladies who keep them minding their manners inside the bar—he pointed at Pauline. Then there's Kristen, though she was born into Bantorus MC, she's now my old lady. Slade's wife Taylor and Raul's old lady Crystal all keep the peace around here. But the single women who only want to be hangers and sleep with the men are bitches. They're not the kind you want to trust in a relationship. The girls know their role while they're on Bantorus land, and mostly follow the rules. Not one of them would go up against an old lady or you, so you won't have any problem with them."

She couldn't help searching for Torque to see if he left with one of the single women. She found him putting the chairs on the tables. "So, that biker earlier who called me a bitch thought I was available?"

"Yeah. His mistake. He won't do that again. I'll have Rain take the subject of you working here to the table when he gets back." Bruce picked up the loaded bin. "Word will get around. Everyone will protect you, and that includes Torque—he stepped out of line tonight, and it won't happen again."

Warmth flooded her neck and she nodded. Her behavior was inexcusable; even more so than Torque's reckless kiss because she was working.

"They also protect the bitches, but there's a fine line that can't be crossed around those in Bantorus MC, and that includes you as Bantorus property seeing as how you're working for Rain. It's called respect." Bruce patted her shoulder as he walked behind her.

Alone behind the bar, she understood what Bruce told her about the way Rain ran the bar. The anarchy wasn't much different than with Los Li. Except here, she wasn't a bitch. Not that she'd chosen to sleep around with any of the members of Los Li, but that's because she could work for them here instead. She picked up the rag on the bar and tossed it in the other bin for dirty laundry. At least within Bantorus MC, the protection they offered her helped settle her nerves.

She went through her tasks to close for the night step by step, and deposited the money in the office the way Rain instructed. In the hall, she yelled, "Bruce, I'm heading out."

Bruce pushed through the swinging doors from the kitchen and held up his hand. "Hang on, and I'll find you a chaperone."

She shook her head. "I'm good. I'll see you tomorrow."

Taylor smiled goodbye and Ginger shrugged and turned away when she waved goodbye to the other employees. She picked up her leather bag out of the backroom and walked out the backdoor. Determined not to let the other girls' attitude bother her, she shook off the coldness left over from their treatment. All they had to do was work together, not become best friends.

Outside, the cool damp air tickled her bare arms. She paused, tilted her face to the sky, and inhaled the fresh air. Running a bar was something she was good at and had come second nature to her. By the time she was eight, she was serving dinner, wiping tables, and pocketing the tips the customers left her while working in her parents' bar. When she reached her teen years, she'd taken over for her mom when she became unable to run the business. Then shit happened, and she put everything she had into keeping her head above water. She scoffed, shaking her head at the turn of events and bad luck.

A motorcyclist rode past her and stopped at the cabin on the end. She walked across the gravel parking lot, ignoring the activity. Once the motorcycle shut off, the sound of footsteps in the gravel behind her came closer. She sped up, not wanting to come face to face with one of the bikers.

"Hey," a male voice said.

She glanced behind her without stopping and found Torque following her. "Work's over and the bar is closed."

He kept coming toward her. Her heart raced. Ten more feet and she'd hit the porch of the cabin. Thankfully, she left the light on like Rain suggested or she'd be stuck out in the dark with Torque.

She had her key out of her pocket and in the lock before Torque joined her on the porch. She squeezed the life out of the handle trying to get inside, but the door wouldn't open even though she'd turned the key.

"Dammit," she muttered, jiggling the handle.

Torque's arm came in front of her and he banged his fist on the door right in front of her at eye level. The door swung open on its own. She exhaled and turned to look at him. "How'd you do that?"

"Doors warped. Press up high and turn the handle at the same time." Torque reached in and flipped the light switch. "It rains a lot here and the doors made out of cheap wood. I'll talk to Rain tomorrow, and have a new door installed."

"Oh, no, that's okay. I'll figure it out." She stepped inside and turned around, blocking him from following her into the cabin. "Was there a reason you followed me home?"

"Just protecting Bantorus property." Torque shoved his hands in his back pockets and stepped off the porch. "Night."

She stood in the doorway, watching him walk away. Unsure if she was impressed with his manners or disappointed that he didn't try to kiss her again, she said, "Hey, Torque."

He turned around not saying a word. She shrugged. "Thanks for, you know, what happened in the bar."

Torque's head tilted. "The kiss?"

She moistened her lips, wanting to smile. "No. For punching that guy who called me a bitch and making him apologize. You didn't have to do that, but it was…nice."

"I'm not nice, sunshine," he said, turning around and this time he kept walking until he disappeared out of view.

She inhaled deeply and closed the door. He was probably right, but she didn't see anyone else standing up for her in the bar or kissing her until she lost her breath. She leaned against the cabin door. Her emotions were playing mind games with her. Normally, she wouldn't be attracted to Torque.

Even though he was gorgeous and bossy in a way that made her feel special for being singled out, she had bigger things to worry about. And she definitely didn't have time to waste thinking about the opposite sex. She tapped the back of her head against the wood, trying to knock some sense into her overstressed head. He might be an asshole, but he'd protected her when it mattered. She had to admit, right or wrong, she needed all the protection she could get.

Chapter Three

After three days of drizzle, the clouds finally parted and the sun warmed the air. Torque grabbed his leather coat off the chair in the lobby of Shift's Garage and pushed his way through the door. Once he arrived at Cactus Cove, he'd have a wet ass from the spray coming off the back tire of his Harley. That and the fact that Brandy would be at the bar soured his mood.

He'd almost succeeded at pushing Brandy out of his head, until last night when he tied on one too many with Remmy and heard the talk about the bets between some of the other Bantorus men who were waiting around for Rain to give his okay for them to make their move on the new manager. Then shit got real.

He used the sleeve of his jacket to swipe the wetness off the seat of his Harley. Water ran in droplets over the edge of the leather. He was ready for sunshine and the calm he found hanging around the bar. This time of year was tough for a biker in the Pacific Northwest. The rain meant less days straddling the bike, and more days inside.

He steeled himself for the onslaught of moisture that remained and sat his bike. Without waiting, he started the engine and pulled out onto the street. Rain would be in the office, and he had to discuss what he planned to do about Brandy and the guys who planned to use her for their own personal challenge.

Bantorus rules forbid anyone, biker, employee, acquaintance, from messing around with Gladys. The rule shouldn't change because Brandy was young, available, and asking for attention.

Five minutes later, he parked his motorcycle in the lot of Cactus Cove and hopped off. He ignored the uncomfortable dampness on his ass and the obvious strip of wetness on his lower back from the road spray, and strode through the backdoor of the bar.

He knocked on the closed office door. He stared at the wood and not down the hallway where Brandy would be.

"Yeah, it's open," Rain said from inside the room.

Torque opened the door and shut it behind him. Not one to waste time, he said, "We've got a problem. The guys are throwing down bets on who can get Brandy first."

Rain let the paper in his hand fall to the desk and leaned back, placing his boots on the corner of the furniture. "It's bullshit talk. They're allowed to let off steam without bothering her."

"Are the rules changing? Gladys was protected, just like any other daughter, sister, mother, old lady is protected." He stepped forward and remained standing. "Brandy's an employee of Bantorus MC."

Rain grinned. "Gladys became an old lady a week after I bought the bar. She remained a Bantorus after Willy was killed. If you haven't noticed, she's in her sixties. Love her to death, but she already played her wild times out and let everyone know she was through spreading her legs. If the same rules apply, then Brandy's free to—"

"You know what I mean. Brandy's, what…twenty-eight—"

"Twenty four," Rain said.

Shit. Twenty four? She had no idea what she was doing at that young of an age.

"I'll talk with her, but I doubt she'll want to throw in with the bitches." Rain put his feet on the floor. "If the men step out of line, I'll deal with it. What's your real problem with Brandy, besides the talk of you sticking your tongue down her throat…which I take isn't going to happen again."

He could give a rat's ass if Rain knew what he did. "She doesn't belong here. Anyone can see she isn't used to being around bikers. How well did you check her out?"

Rain stood. "Are you questioning my decision? Because the last time I looked, I owned the fucking bar."

"Right." Torque scoffed.

Rain rounded the desk and sat on the top in front of Torque. "You've been through a lot the last year and I know shit piles on you, so I'll ignore the asshole in you coming out. Do you need time away? Bantorus has a run coming up, and it'll take two weeks. I'm trying to set up an agreement to transport cars down to Lagsturns on a regular schedule."

Torque braced. "Chops?"

"Not on our end. What they do with them afterward, it's not on our back." Rain studied him. "That bother you?"

There was no question that Lagsturns Motorcycle Club would use the cars in an illegal activity and send them back on the road containing parts of stolen vehicles. Torque shook his head. "No problem."

He had no love for the outlaw motorcycle club, and preferred to stay far away from them and anyone doing business with them. The last time he played too close, Los Li shot him on two separate occasions. Dealing with anyone who went into business with Los Li, a gang formed in the penal system in California under the leadership of the Mexican mafia, was bad news.

"Are you up for the job?" Rain asked again.

He'd like nothing more than to take a break and come back with his head screwed on straight. Though it was having his thoughts in the wrong place lately that could affect his judgment and put Bantorus at risk. "Let Remmy take the run. I'll pull his shift at the garage."

As Sergeant at Arms to his president, he floated between club business and wherever Rain needed him on the outside. He enjoyed the lifestyle. Whether he was doing construction at the hotel, fixing cars at the garage, or repo'ing vehicles for non-payment, the array of jobs within Bantorus MC community kept him busy and away from growing stagnant.

"Good." Rain clapped his hand on Torque's shoulder. "Why don't you talk to Tori in the next couple of days?"

"Why?" he asked.

Rain shrugged. "She's worried about you. You know how she gets when something bothers her."

"There's nothing going on for her to get wound up," he said.

"Tell that to my old lady." Rain's grin disappeared. "Don't bullshit around what's going on. I've known you over twenty years. I've watched you, worried about you, and fought with you. You're heading into a dark place, which is understandable considering what you went through. Bantorus is here. Hang on to us, and keep your head. You're a free man."

Rain wasn't giving him advice, but an order. He'd sank low, fighting to outrun his past and letting anger build, enough in past years that he was given round the clock watch. After the fact, he hated having his brothers involved in his personal life. Not one of them knew why he continued to fight demons, except Rain. He could handle his past on his own. That's the reason he refused to settle down like Rain or Slade or the other members who put their care into someone else's hand. He didn't want anyone's help.

"Tell Tori I'll stop by the house tomorrow, and see her and Lilly." He cleared his throat, turned for the door.

If there was one person who helped him just by being in the same room, it was Tori. Her calmness and nurturing came from the heart, despite the hell she'd lived through growing up. Hell, her goodness penetrated every hardened member in the club.

A knock, followed by the office door opening and Brandy sticking her head inside, stopped Torque from leaving. He stepped back and regretted looking the second Brandy's eyes fell on him.

Her cheeks flushed. The base of her neck pulsed and he found his own blood pumping faster at the sight of her reaction.

"Sorry. I didn't know anyone was in here." Brandy raked her teeth over her bottom lip. "I'll come back."

"Brandy," Rain said, stopping her from going anywhere. "Stay."

Torque moved toward the door to go past Brandy, and Rain said. "Torque, stick around."

He clamped his teeth and stayed planted beside Brandy. He hated how he wanted to lift his chin at Rain and accept anything he asked if only to stay in Brandy's presence. She was a baby compared to him. Hell, he had nineteen years on her. He'd already fucked up his life before she was even born.

"Torque mentioned there was talk going around the bar, by some Bantorus members, about you." Rain lowered his voice. "I promised you safety here, and every one of the men will be held to the same promise not to bother you. Talk is talk, and as long as it remains talk, you're going to have to deal with it."

Brandy's chin lifted. "I have no complaints."

Enough pussyfooting around the truth, Torque wanted her to know how serious the men were on making her a bitch. "They're taking bets on who will get in your panties first."

Brandy gaze came to him and she blinked up at him. "That almost sounds as if everyone assumes I wear panties."

Rain laughed, breaking the tension in the room. "Then that's settled."

"Awesome." Brandy grinned. "I came in here to ask if you knew anyone who could take a look at my car. I know you own the garage, but I don't want to make an appointment and waste anyone's time if this turns out to be nothing. I just bought the car two weeks before I moved here to take the job, so maybe the noise coming from the front is normal. There's a knocking…sort of tinny sound when I push the pedal."

Rain nodded. "I'll run it over to the garage—"

"I'll take a look at it." Torque stepped forward. "It's probably something I can fix in the parking lot."

"Right." Rain motioned to the door, gazing at Brandy. "Take an hour off and show Torque what's going on with your cage. I'll cover the bar."

"But I've already taken my lunch break." Brandy pressed her hand against her stomach. "I should stay here and—"

"Come on. Clock's ticking." Torque placed his hand flat on her lower back and guided her out of the room, down the hall, and out the back door. "Which one's yours?"

She frowned at him, but pointed at the far edge of the lot. "The black Cadillac."

"Figures," he muttered, dropping his hand and walking in front of her.

"What's that mean?" She hurried to catch up with him. "It's a decent car."

"Sure it is," he said. "But no single girl drives a cage like that."

The black glossy paint and lift couldn't hide the fact that the car was two years old at most. He walked around the front bumper, trailing his hand across the hood, pausing where the hood ornament was missing. His fingers rolled into his palms and he scanned the area for anything out of the ordinary. There was only one reason why someone would take off a Cadillac's hood ornament.

"Where did you buy the car?" he asked.

"Um. I got it when I lived in Cali…Wayne's Car Emporium, I think." She leaned her hip against the fender. "Why? Is something wrong? I'm still making payments and I swear, since I arrived in Pitnam something feels *off* with the car. I hope I didn't buy a lemon."

He watched her for any little movement or hesitation, but she simply waited for him to continue. What were the odds that Brandy had no idea why the sight of the caddy had him breaking out in a sweat?

He forced his teeth apart to continue. "It's a drug runner."

"What do you mean?" She stepped closer.

He slipped off his vest, folded the leather in half, and set it on the hood of her car. "Whoever owned the Cadillac before you had gang affiliation. What part of the state did you come from?"

"California. South Beach area." She frowned. "That's creepy, but the car lot I bought it at was legit. It's my car now, or will be when I'm done paying for it."

He kneeled down and rolled onto his back. Scooting his way under the car, he skipped the usual areas to look for problems with knocking, and checked the underside carriage for a tracker. When he was sure the car was clean, he rolled out from underneath and stood. "You land in Bantorus territory driving a car I'd bet my bike came from a member of Los Li, dressed like a bitch, getting in my face, and stand there all innocent. Why don't you come clean now? If you're lucky Rain will let you leave the territory in your shiny car."

"What are you talking about?" She pushed his chest, trying to scoot him away from her. "Why are you crowding me?"

Until she laid her hands on him, he hadn't realized he'd stepped up against her, pinning her to the car. He gazed down in her eyes. "You dress hotter than dual chrome plated exhaust pipes, shoving your nose in the air and yet stand here defending your choice of a new car. I don't know how you got past Rain, but your gigs over."

Her brows pinched. "What are you accusing me of? Buying a used car? Needing a job?"

Her bottom lip trembled and tears welled in her eyes, though she blinked to hide them. He cupped her neck, holding her in front of him. The soft strands of her hair slid between his fingers. He inhaled deeply. She smelled better than whiskey.

"Stop the charade." He leaned his lower half against her. "Someone got you the job, and I want to know who."

"N-nobody." Her breath tickled his lips. "I went through an agency. Ask Rain if you don't believe me."

He brushed his mouth against hers. "Boyfriend?"

"No," she whispered, arching her neck and giving him access to her lips.

His free hand went to her ass, pulling her snug between his thighs. "Bitch?"

"No," she said on an exhale. "I'm nobody's bitch."

"Good answer, sunshine." He captured her lips.

Unlike the other night when he'd taken the kiss from her, he softened his lips, taking possession of her emotions he'd placed on her. He soothed the trembles, tasted the fear, and breathed the heat forming between them. He celebrated in her hesitation, proving she was telling the truth. He controlled every move, and she gave herself to him willingly.

He stroked her tongue, sucking hers into his mouth. His cock hardened and he held her perfectly molded against him. Her body relaxed, and he took her weight. Holding her was like having power over his fears, his worries, his freedom. The closer she came, the more confident he became. He could handle her, handle the feelings, and handle the consequences of messing around with her.

She sucked his bottom lip, pulling away gently, panting. He tilted her head and looked down in her eyes, swept away from the startling clarity staring back at him.

"I don't know what you're trying to do with me," she said.

He inhaled, not letting her go. "If you were smart, you'd run back into the bar."

"And if I don't want to?" she whispered.

He kissed her lightly, still reeling from wanting her and knowing he had to be the one who put a stop to what they were doing. "Choice isn't yours."

The need to stay where he was and continue to enjoy the touch of a woman left him shaky. He forced himself to let go and step back. "You have the keys with you?"

"The what?" She put her hand to her mouth.

"The keys to the car, sunshine." He grinned, enjoying her aroused confused and knowing he was the one who put her in that condition.

She pulled a single key with a red ribbon out of her pocket. "Yeah."

He took the makeshift keychain from her and opened the door. "I'll drive it around the block and listen for the noise. Go ahead and go inside. I might need to take it onto I-5 and get the engine temperature hotter to hear the knocking."

"Okay." She nodded, but continued standing there. After several seconds, she said, "Torque?"

"Yeah?" He brought his attention back around to her.

She worked her hands in worry. "Nevermind. It's not important."

She walked away. He watched her long strides take her inside the bar. When he was alone, he punched the steering wheel.

He might not know what he was doing in the next hour when it came to Brandy, but he sure in the hell knew he wasn't going to let any other man touch her. She gave him everything in a kiss, and he was damned well going to make sure she only gave that to him.

He started the car. There was only one way to get her out of his head. He'd show her what kind of trouble she'd get into if she stuck around. The way she reacted to their kiss, he'd be between her legs in no time and she'd run away scared. He'd finally be free of his problem where Brandy was concerned.

Chapter Three

Brandy pressed her back against the wall in the hallway after leaving Torque outside with her car and thrust both hands into her hair, holding her head. What was she doing?

Oh my God.

Torque knew she was driving a Los Li car. He'd taken one look and called her out. Lies rolled off her tongue faster than she could stop them, and if she went by the kiss Torque gave her, he believed every messed up thing she said.

Radiant had to have known someone from Bantorus would question her about the car. Why would he set her up that way if he wanted her to gain information?

She fisted her hair, wanting to scream.

Then Torque had kissed her. Again.

Petrified she'd give herself away, she kissed him back. She closed her eyes and groaned. God, she was a liar. She wanted to kiss him, but that made her the very thing he accused her of being. She was not a bitch.

She'd had a few dates, but most of her experience came from a handful of one-night stands when she managed to go out after work. Five one-night stands to be exact. Not a number that made her a habitual slut. Lately, she couldn't even find time for herself.

"Hey." Bruce walked out of the supply room. "Everything okay?"

"Yeah." She dropped her hands and gave him a smile bordering on a grimace. "No. It's my car. Torque's looking at it, but I'm having buyer's remorse. I think I bought a piece of crap. So much for purchasing on looks alone."

Bruce shrugged her concern away. "If Torque's working on it, he'll have the cage up and running in no time. He's good with anything that has an engine."

She only had a uterus and ovaries, but he definitely had a way to get things running. She pushed off the wall. "You're right. I'm not going to worry about it. When I get the final diagnoses, then I'll worry."

She and Bruce walked back to the bar together. The dinner crowd slowly trickled in. She busied herself taking inventory of glasses and the contents of the freezer. Last night she also noticed that Bruce was doing double time running the industrial size dishwasher in the back of the kitchen, which took valuable time away from customers ordering drinks.

When she finished averaging the usage of dishes with the quantity of food going out, she approached Ginger. "Can I speak with you a moment?"

"Yeah." Ginger slipped her pen in the pocket of her cutoffs.

"I'd like you and Taylor to switch on and off taking the bins of glasses to the dishwasher and loading everything. I'll cover your tables while you're gone," Brandy said.

"You're kidding?" Ginger planted her hand on her hip. "That's crazy."

Brandy shook her head. "No, it's one task that pulls Bruce away from the counter. We don't want to make the customers wait for their drinks. It'd be easier if the wait crew divided the job, since there's only one bartender here at a time we'll take turns with the chore."

Ginger motioned over Brandy's shoulder. "Tell this chick I'm not doing the dishes."

Laughter came from behind her. Brandy turned around and found two bikers—Jedman and Pete shaking their head in amusement. She turned back to Ginger and lowered her voice. "When I'm talking to you, it's a private conversation. My request wasn't unreasonable, and in your job description papers you signed—which I've read front to back—any duties directed toward the waitresses will be directed by the managerial staff. That's me."

"Listen here, *Brandy*." Ginger glared. "You want me to do something, you ask Rain to inform me. Not you."

"Is there a problem with taking requests from me?" She raised her brows to make a point. "I'd be happy to have us both sit down with Rain and discuss the matter in a professional manner."

Ginger's nostrils flared. "I'll save you the trouble—she called out to Rain and motioned for him—just ask Rain yourself."

Rain stepped up beside Brandy. "Ginger…?"

"Tell her, I don't do dishes." Ginger folded her arms under her breasts.

Rain glanced between Brandy and Ginger. "Brandy, the girls had an agreement worked out with Gladys that they wouldn't work in the kitchen. You can honor the standing verbal terms or make your own. That's why I hired you."

"Rain," Ginger said. "You can't let her push us around."

"She's the manager." He turned around, putting the authority back in Brandy's hands.

Ginger sighed loudly and remained quiet. Brandy watched Rain walk away, leaving her to decide whether she wanted to push her idea or back down. She'd worked too many years with girls exactly like Ginger who learned how to manipulate to get what they wanted. Strong, independent girls who had learned to endure from a young age. Servers used everything they had to put money in their pocket and keep a roof over their heads. She wasn't any different.

She'd scraped to support herself and her dad running their bar and fought for every right that came her way out of responsibility and survival. Ginger wasn't going to give up easily.

Ginger set her chin at a high angle and waited her out. Brandy gave nothing away. "I like what Gladys has done and how she combined work ethics with a personal connection with the working staff, but there's room for improvement. I understand you've gone from a four-waitperson team down to two. Both you and Taylor are putting in double shifts while Rain interviews for one more full time employee and a couple of part timers."

"No one is complaining about the double shift," Ginger stated.

She nodded. "Not yet, but there's ways we can improve. Bruce can't be taking the time to take the bins back to the kitchen, loading and unloading the dishwasher. The extra job pulls him away from the customers, which leaves more people at the tables waiting for service. That means—"

"Hold on. Are you accusing—?"

"*That* means customers are hanging around the bar longer, taking up a table that'd serve someone else. It also means the longer they have to stay in the bar to get their buzz on, the more likelihood that you're getting out of here at three in the morning, instead of two," Brandy said.

Several seconds ticked by, and then Ginger's mouth curved into a smile. "Like an assembly line. The faster we serve, the sooner we get done."

"And the more tips land in your tight little shorts." Brandy grinned. "Win-Win."

Ginger's arms unfolded and her shoulders dropped in relaxation. "I hear you on that, girlfriend. Count me in on doing the dishwasher. I'll talk to Taylor when she comes in, but I know she'll do anything if it means extra money. She and Slade are trying to save up to buy a bigger house for the kids."

"Great. I'll also help with the dishwasher duties. If we all take turns when we have a few moments to spare, it won't seem like such a chore." Brandy stepped back and motioned for her to go back to work. "Thanks for talking with me."

Ginger shrugged. "You're all right. Not a Gladys, but you'll do."

She smiled. Inside she pumped her fist and laughed hysterically in success. Her first obstacle now behind her, she celebrated at getting past Ginger's cold treatment toward her and having her see them as equals working together for a good cause. She wasn't looking for friends, and even though her job was a cover for whatever reason Los Li wanted her inside the hubbub of Bantorus MC, she was going to do the best damn job she could do.

"Nice work," a deep voice said behind her.

Her adrenaline congregated in her lower stomach. Knowing the caressing voice, she turned around more eager to see him than she wanted to let him know. "Hey, Torque."

His gaze studied her face, then lowered and swept the length of her body, cementing her to the spot. She couldn't move if she wanted to, and the last thing she wanted to do is move away and lose what he gave her every time he was near. Her feelings were crazy and unrealistic, but she couldn't tell her body not to want more from him.

He seemed content to look at her, but she had to get back to work. She couldn't expect everyone else to step up and do extra work if she stood around gawking at one of the bikers. "Did you need something?"

He stepped forward until her breasts, already sensitive and aware of him, brushed his chest. His hand slipped into her front pocket of her jeans. She gasped. His touch, so close to her sex, stole her next breath.

His lips softened, letting her know he could see right through her. "Cars fixed."

"W-what was wrong with it?" she asked, not moving away.

His other hand landed on her hip and he pulled her tighter against him. He said on a contented exhale, "Timing belt."

Her chest constricted and her body pulsed. "How much do I owe you?"

"More than you're willing to give me." He held on to her, but his gaze went over her head. "I'll call us even if you stand right there and let me hold you."

"That's all?" She gazed up into his unreadable face.

He had no idea she wanted to pay the price. She'd take a high interest loan out with a bank to finance her way into bed with him.

"Yep," he whispered, dipping his head and inhaling. "You, your body, your smell, your tight jeans, and…damn, those boots."

She leaned against him. "I need to work."

"I know that, sunshine." His chest expanded and he squeezed the slope of her hip. "I also know you only have a couple of hours left and you get off before the dinner crowd arrives."

She shook her head, trying to clear the lustful fog surrounding her and think about what he was telling her. "Yeah, Rain's working tonight and tomorrow's my day off."

She couldn't understand why he'd want to discuss her work schedule. The impassive attitude he had a few hours ago no longer existed, and he almost sounded as if he was interested in what she did in her free time.

"Be outside your cabin after work." He stepped away. "Be there."

He looked away, lifted his chin to Bruce at the bar, and then walked down the hallway. She stared after him long past the time that she lost sight of him. Something about him was different. Not only had his antagonism toward her changed. He seemed more relaxed…open.

Chapter Four

The girls in the last cabin in the row behind the door opened their door for business. Torque gazed at the hanger pausing on the porch with brown hair and a set of hips made for a man's hands. He contemplated walking over and having her relieve him of the hard-on he sported thanks to Brandy. However, he wasn't in the mood for one of the Bantorus girls or the back and forth dance that was required.

Hell, most of the hangers had their own apartment or rental house in Pitnam, but used the cabin to hang out in hopes he or a few of the other guys would pay them a visit. If the girls could raise their head in the morning and get outside at a decent time, Rain would often hand out jobs at the hotel in housekeeping or deliveries for the garage. But a job was a bonus to them. They stayed close to Cactus Cove for the attention and knowing someone was watching out for them.

Excess energy made his steps lighter as he made his way to his bike. He only had a couple of hours to wait until Brandy was off work. The anticipation of having Brandy underneath him was worth the agonizing sweetness of being ready to have sex with her tonight.

Forgoing the helmet strapped to the bitch seat on his Harley, he straddled the bike. He'd check in at the garage, figure out his schedule for tomorrow, and work around spending time with Brandy. One of the guys would change shifts with him if needed.

A night and half of a day would be enough to get Brandy out of his head.

A loud whistle brought his head up. Slade jogged toward him. He swung his leg off the bike and waited for his Bantorus brother.

Slade didn't stop as he approached and slammed Torque against the brick wall of the bar with his vest crumpled in Slade's fists. Slade got in his face. "What the hell are you doing?"

Torque shoved Slade off him. He'd like nothing more than fight. "Go ahead, hit me."

"You asshole," Slade muttered, slinging his arm around Torque's neck in a familiar camaraderie. "Take a ride and even out before you step too far over the line"

"I know what I'm doing." He tensed, rejecting the reminder about club rules.

"Stay away from her." Slade shook his head. "Don't use her, or you'll put yourself up against Rain."

"Rain's good, man," Torque said. "Nothing's going to happen that can't happen."

His good mood stayed despite Slade's advice meant to tap him down. He had everything under control. Nothing was going to stop him. Brandy was there for the taking, and he wanted her. Hell, he could've had her on the floor of the bar, while she was working. She was that into him.

"Hey, why don't you come on over tonight. Taylor's fixing dinner. We'll have a few beers, shoot some pool in the garage," Slade said.

"Got things to do, man." Torque play punched Slade in the stomach.

"Torque…" Slade's arm fell away from him and his jaw twitched. "Talk to me."

He laughed. Sometimes the guys were a bunch of oversensitive babies.

"Nothing to say. I'm not scheduled to work today, and—hey, do you know if I'm on the books to work tomorrow?" he said.

"Yeah. Pete's got you and me down to work," Slade said.

"Damn." He shook his head. "Can't do it. I'll call Remmy and have him come in."

Slade widened his stance. "You need to work and to stay away from the new manager. Rules, brother."

Torque hopped on his Harley. "Don't worry about what I do…and lighten up. Go grab Taylor and work off some of that stress you're carrying around, or I will have to punch you."

He rode off, leaving Slade in the parking lot. He needed Brandy worse than he needed the money he'd get for working. The way she reacted in the bar, he'd have no problems keeping her satisfied.

After flagging down Remmy at the garage, promising him a case of beer and two weekend exchanges, he'd cleared everything from his schedule tomorrow. His night and day were free. To waste time before going back to the bar to meet Brandy, he headed out of town.

Opening his throttle, he sailed past the cars on I-5. Nothing could catch him with the wind in his face and his responsibilities behind him.

Fuck his dad.

Fuck his life.

Fuck the time wasted, the darkness, the caged feeling that he could never quite shake.

He stretched his legs, sliding his boots off the pegs. He'd outran his past long ago, but when he least expected it, the panic of all those years wasted crippled him.

Turning off the exit, he remembered the promised stop to talk with Tori. He calculated the distance he'd already covered, and how long it'd normally take him to make it back to Cactus Cove, and forced a quick turn on in the middle of the road to go to his president's house. If he kept Tori from talking his ear off, he'd make good time and be back at Brandy's cabin to meet her after work.

When he approached the street where he had to slow down and turn, he passed Rain heading toward town on his motorcycle. He held out his arm, two fingers spread wide, and got the same sign from Rain. He arrived at the house and hopped off the bike.

"You just missed Rain." Tori stood on the porch and planted her hands on her hips. "Where's your helmet?"

"Bike." He hitched his thumb over his shoulder and walked up the steps. "Don't lecture."

"Then don't be stupid with your life." She swatted his arm before patting his chest in friendship. "Did you come to see me?"

He grinned, unable to stop, because he'd never met a woman who always seemed surprised that others enjoyed spending time with her. "Yeah."

"Good. Come on in, but be quiet. I just put Lilly down for a nap. She's thinks she's too old to sleep and threw the biggest fit until Rain laid down with her. Then she collapsed," Tori hooked her long blonde hair behind her ear and opened the door.

Lilly, Rain and Tori's only child, had both her parents' undivided attention at almost two years old. She was also a splitting image of her mom, which had Rain bullshitting nonsense when anyone mentioned his daughter's name. He was happy for Rain and Tori, though he couldn't understand giving up his freedom and settling down with one woman, despite how highly he respected Tori.

He sat down on the couch in the large living room overlooking the Lewis River. "Rain said you wanted to see me."

"Of course, I do. You haven't been by, and I haven't had time to try to find you." Tori pulled her legs up underneath her in the chair across from him. "How're you doing?"

"Working most days. Bike's running. Bills are paid, so I can say life's pretty damn good," Torque said.

"You know that's not what I'm talking about," Tori said, and it was the concern he heard in her voice that had him looking away.

"I'm good." He shrugged. "The muscles are a little tight in the morning, but after a couple of hours working at the garage, my shoulder loosens up."

He was lucky to be alive. That's what everyone kept telling him. He still wasn't sure the scars were worth worrying about. His recovery had taken time, but he could still ride a bike and that's all that mattered to him.

"No more flashbacks?" Tori asked, not pulling any punches.

He stood and walked to the sliding door. Only one woman came around when he was recovering, and Tori made sure he was comfortable and well cared for. Taylor, who was admitted to the hospital at the same time, never mentioned the shooting after making sure he was okay upon her release. Not because she didn't care, she cared too much. He tried to keep his distance, because he'd seen the haunted look in her eyes whenever they were around each other. He respected both women probably more than he respected any man.

He accepted and understood Taylor's choice to move on and not discuss what'd happened. Things could've turned out differently for everyone, and he accepted what happened. Better him than Rain or Slade, who both had families to look after.

Tori and Rain spent many nights with him after he got home from the hospital, supporting and taking care of him. He couldn't hide his panic and unease when the doctors had him drugged up and riding high. He'd used the closest thing he had available to cover up the truth and blamed his behavior on the shootings.

He was good at making excuses. They had no idea his conduct ran back to his time in prison, or that his anger wasn't over what Los Li did to him. He was born into the wrong family. He had a rap sheet longer than his arm and although he was forty-three years old, he'd only spent the last twenty years a free man.

Keeping his freedom was important, and his biggest fear.

"Nope. It's in the past. My days are good, like I was telling you; nothing bothers me except a little stiffness in my shoulder in the morning." He turned around and grinned. "I need to get out of here. There's someone waiting for me. Give Lilly a kiss from her Uncle Torque and make sure Rain brings you around to the club."

Tori got to her feet and walked him to the door. "One of the girls for the club or someone new?"

He half turned, and kissed her forehead. "I don't slap jack. Go pester one of the other guys about their sex life, huh?"

"You're no fun." Tori laughed. "You're just afraid I'll end up putting your life in my column in the newspaper."

Torque shook his head and walked out the door. He waved over his shoulder as he continued down the steps to his bike. Rain was a lucky bastard, but hc had his hands full with his old lady.

They'd gone through hell and despite the shit Tori went through as a child, she came out balanced. It was Tori's balancing act and ability to move on with life that continued to escape him with his own life. She'd never understand how he had no control, but then again, he wouldn't give her a chance to take on his problems too.

The sun slipped behind the hills. He flipped on his headlight and cruised the back road to Pitnam. More sedate than he was earlier, he pushed the speed limit to get to Brandy before he wound down.

As he pulled into the parking lot of Cactus Cove, his timing perfect, he spotted Brandy halfway to her cabin. Bypassing his normal parking spot, he rode to the back and cut her off in front of her porch.

Brandy slung her purse over her shoulder, and stood in front of him taking him all in. He cut the engine and put the kickstand down, but stayed on the motorcycle.

Her chest rose and fell, and she sucked in her breath and caught her lower lip between her teeth. His balls tightened in pleasure. For the first time, she appeared vulnerable and indecisive to him. He enjoyed knowing he had that effect on her.

He moved off the bike, gathered her hand, and strode to the cabin with her. When she stalled, holding the key, he unlocked the door for her. He'd given her a couple of hours to think about what was going to happen, to change her mind, to leave Bantorus land. She'd made her decision.

Inside, she dropped her purse and curled into hm. Her arms went around him in a hug. Taken aback, he waited and tried to slow his racing heart. This tenderness, this move, this change in what he expected to happen set him back.

Instead of lifting her face to kiss him, she laid her cheek against his chest. He sank his hands into her hair, surprised to find them shaking. He was used to women stripping off their clothes, tearing off his, or falling to their knees to blow him off.

What he expected to happen between them wasn't happening. He gazed down at the top of her head. He had no idea what she was doing to him.

Sweat broke out on his forehead. His cock pulsed pleasurably, and yet he made no move to go forward and take her on the floor. For some reason, he wanted to remain right here, doing nothing.

No one had ever held him before that he could remember. Awkward and foreign to him, he tried to figure out why a hug brought him a sense of security when he usually only found himself wanting to push the boundaries and take everything he could from a woman wanting to have sex with him. He came up empty. Therefore, he stood there and did nothing.

Chapter Five

Brandy's whole body vibrated. Between the hyperaware condition Torque had left her in at the bar and worrying about when Radiant would contact her, she warred with what to do now that Torque was here.

Fear settled around her.

Fear of being yanked away from Cactus Cove without any warning, any chance to see Torque again, any hope of finding her dad. All day, surrounded by bikers, dealing with the threat of Los Li and at the mercy of Radiant's command, she clung to the one person who told her to stay away from him.

She was insane.

Insane, because there was no doubt in her mind that she'd have sex with him. From the moment he stared at her across the parking lot on her first day working, something about him reinforced her opinion that he was the only one she could trust.

She trembled against the solid wall of biker in front of her, soaking in his warmth.

Her hormones bounced up and down, leaving her out of whack. Her self-control knew no boundaries. She wanted Torque, any way she could have him…and the insanity that drove her into his arms scared her.

"Sunshine," Torque said, arching his back while lifting her chin. "What's going on?"

"I want you," she blurted.

Desperate to keep things even between them, at the most basic level, and needing to keep him from asking too many questions, she slid her hands up his chest. Her fingers curled around the edges of his hair brushing his shoulders. Unable to reach his mouth, she tugged on him as she stretched to her tiptoes and kissed him.

She slipped her tongue into his mouth, and his hand circled the back of her neck, through her hair, and pulled her away. He glared down at her. "No."

She opened her mouth to ask him what was wrong, and he kissed her. His tongue stroked hers, taking, and dominating her. The aggression surprised and delighted her. Her body melted into his capable hands. He took away her indecisiveness and allowed her to accept whatever he wanted to do to her without any responsibility.

He held her tight, bending her body to his will. Her breasts pulsed. Her sex dampened. Emotions relaxed her throat, and she hung on to Torque to keep from losing herself. He created a maelstrom of feelings throughout every inch of her that had nothing to do with should she or shouldn't she have sex with him.

She was definitely going to have sex. At this moment, that's all she needed.

Then she was in Torque's arms, her feet off the floor, her head cradled in the palm of his hand. Her muscles warmed and relaxed. The whole time he carried her to the bedroom, he continued kissing her. There was nothing required of her, but to accept what he was doing to her.

He placed her on the bed, followed her down, and lay on top of her. Her legs gave way to his weight and he settled against her sex. At the brush of his body, she frantically reached for him.

He stilled. "No."

She held on to his biceps, lost in what was happening to make his body harden—and not in a good way. She wanted to have sex. He wanted to have sex. She could feel the proof of his arousal between her legs.

"What did I do?" she said, or maybe she only thought the question because he never answered.

He pushed her top up over her breasts, pulled down her bra, and latched on to her nipple. Electric jolts seared her core. His tongue caressed the sensitive bud, alternating between a hard suck and lavishing attention on her. She arched off the bed, needing and wanting more.

Torque's hands moved to her arms, drawing her hands out to the sides, until she posed on the mattress like a sacrificial peace offering. He lifted his head. The coldness of the room brushed her breast where his moist mouth had been, and she trembled as her nipples constricted into a tight bundle of nerves that picked up Torque's warm breath.

"Keep your hands on the bed and don't move." He moved down her body until he stood on the floor.

He pulled off her boots and tossed them to the floor. She watched every move, afraid if she sat up or went to him, he'd stop. Stopping wasn't an option. She wanted him to go faster, but he continued taking his time.

Torque undid her zipper. She shivered. The *trill* of the teeth coming undone reminded her of how Torque used his teeth to rasp over her bottom lip yesterday, and how much she liked when he kissed her without any restraint.

He undid the button on her jeans and tugged. She lifted her hips, and laid back down, bare from the scrunched shirt under her armpits down to the tip of her toes. He held out his hand, pulled her into a sitting position, and finished undressing her. Perfectly capable of removing her clothes herself, the wait tortured her. She was a bundle of nerves, sensitive to every movement, every breath, every look coming from Torque.

She swallowed hard. The thought of him doing what he's doing to her, but on one of the women who stayed a few cabins down from hers constricted her throat. She closed her eyes, hiding from the truth.

"Hey," he whispered huskily, hovering over her. "Look at me."

She nodded slightly and opened her eyes. "Please don't stop?"

His eyes warmed and for the second time, she noticed a shift in his demeanor. She relaxed her hands, letting her fingers straighten. She pushed why she wanted to please him out of her thoughts, and concentrated on what he was doing.

It was a one-night stand.

It was only sex.

It was safer with Torque than in reality.

He removed a condom from the wallet attached to the chain on his belt. She lifted her arm and stroked the flame running over his chest and onto his neck. His muscles tensed, and a low crooning sound came from his throat. She removed her hand and placed it back on the bed. That didn't stop her from looking instead.

Two rough spherical scars marked his left side below his shoulder at the top of his chest. The edges of the injuries stood out red against his tanned skin. She inhaled deeply, because the wounds looked angry and tender. Suddenly, his refusal to let her touch him made sense. He'd been hurt. He wanted to protect his shoulder.

"Eyes on me." He shoved his jeans down.

She snapped her gaze to his face. "You're hurt."

His brows lowered and he studied her. Finally, he said, "About eleven months ago. I'm fine."

"It looks so—"

"It's fine." He pushed her legs farther apart. "Wet and ready."

"God, yes," she whispered.

He put his hardness to the opening of her sex and slid inside of her in one thrust. Her whole body tensed, not in shock, not in discomfort, not in fear. All her crazy, unpredictable feelings multiplied at once carrying her away. She panted, trying to catch her breath over her pulsating body. Her muscles warmed and spasmed, squeezing and rejoicing.

Clutching the worn bedspread underneath her, she braced against the need to grind her pelvis against him. "Oh God, please."

She needed fast, hard, relief. Instead, Torque slowly pulled out of her until he was barely in her wetness. She squirmed, and he sank back inside of her. Her eyelids fluttered and she fought to keep looking at him. She wanted to moan and thrash on the bed, but she remained perfectly still, letting Torque do everything.

"All sunshine and happy," he muttered, thrusting in, pulling out, stroking her from the inside, and setting her body on fire.

Torque controlled the moment. Her nipples constricted and her skin tingled She relied on him to keep going and bring her pleasure. At his mercy, instead of feeling vulnerable, she basked in knowing he'd satisfy her.

That confidence in another person's ability she received from him was better than anything she'd ever experienced. For as long as she could remember, she was the one responsible to keep her parents moving forward. The only one held accountable for the other employees, the customers, the bills. For years, she'd wanted to escape.

Torque lowered his head and took her breast in his mouth. She bit down on her lip, and even trying to stop the moan from coming out of her thrilled her. She greedily participated by giving Torque what he needed, total control. In return, she got more than she would even know to ask for.

No responsibility, no demands, no pressure to perform.

He forced her to only feel, and suspended time. Her worries evaporated, her security was right here on the bed with him, and he had her undivided attention. He'd done the impossible, and she wasn't going to waste what he was giving her.

Torque balanced on one arm and touched her between the legs without missing a stroke with his cock inside of her. She screamed in pleasure, bucking against him. All over, deep inside of her, every single inch, tightened, heated, spiraled.

The perfect pleasure intensified, and she couldn't stop. She dug her heels into the mattress as her body bowed on the bed. Torque continued plunging into her wetness, mumbling something she was past hearing.

Orgasmic spasms rocked her from deep in her lower stomach, her chest, and out to her fingertips. A flood of wonderful swept through her legs.

During her climax, Torque set his own rhythm, frantic and powerful. He kept her body reacting. Each thrust a caress, sending her deeper into herself.

Then he grunted, plunging fully inside of her and holding still. His dark eyes, vulnerable and passionate, soothed her. She shivered, lowering her hips onto the bed. She couldn't look away. For all purposes, she knew nothing about the man between her legs. He was a stranger, a biker, and in his words an asshole.

Torque's fervent emotions came from having sex. She knew that. She wasn't naïve.

But, as she laid there soaking in everything that had happened since they stepped foot into the cabin, she recognized the real Torque behind the gruff words, the leather vest, the hot body, the badass motorcycle. She was seeing a side of Torque that she suspected he kept carefully hidden. Now that he'd shown her that side of him, she wanted to know what caused the haunted fear shining in his eyes.

Chapter Six

Brandy gazed up at him with the softest, most beautiful smile. He struggled to catch his breath. He'd wanted power over her and when she gave total control to him without any reservations; he didn't know what to do. *Jesus.*

Her attention, her passion, her trust laid in his hands. His heart still raced. He never expected to take her choices away, but she'd handed them over to him like a damn gift.

Torque pushed himself off the bed, took the condom off, and tossed it in the wastebasket by the dresser. He should never have returned to the bar or Brandy.

She nearly killed him when she'd climaxed. He'd never had a woman who came undone and let herself go, with him, because of him, for him.

He'd known all along that she wasn't a bitch. He'd used her, and she didn't deserve a fly by fuck. His chest tightened, and he found himself struggling for a lungful of air. He warned her away, because he was desperate enough to take everything good about her if she stayed.

The room closed in on him. First Slade interrogated him, and then Tori let him know she was concerned about him. He should've known what he was doing. No matter how closed in he became, sex always pitched him the other way.

For the last twenty years, he'd used women, riding, and drink to even life out for him and make him forget the past. They were his medication, his downer on his up days and his uppers on his down days. He looped his belt through the front of his jeans and fastened the buckle. Shit, he had to leave the cabin. No, he *had* to leave Brandy.

A spring on the bed creaked. He stepped toward the opened door and before he could escape, Brandy's hand touched his back. He stopped, his body going into full-blown denial. "Sex, sunshine. That's all it was."

"Yeah," she whispered, dropping her hand. "I know."

Her understanding and sweet voice left him drowning. She was all sunshine and happy for a man living in a dark world.

He forced himself to keep looking forward while he walked to the front door and let himself out. The cool night dried the perspiration on his face, his neck, his arms. He continued walking. He almost wishing Brandy would've yelled or even hit him for how he treated her. The reasons why bothered him more than having sex with her. For the first time, he felt ugly and unfeeling. Something that never bothered him before.

Usually guilt escaped him. He'd ride the high, and leave before he ever settled his mind. Something happened back there when she'd hugged him. Her arms calmed him, and cleared his head. He enjoyed himself too much. What they shared seemed too similar to what always remained out of his grasp, and he was never allowed to have, and that made seeing Brandy again dangerous.

"Hey." Rain whistled, lifting his chin.

Torque took in Rain's location and without turning around to see if the cabin was in view, he knew his game was over. He veered over to the sidewalk and met Rain at the side of the building, knowing exactly what was going to happen. "What's up?"

"Everyone comes to the table tomorrow at three." Rain glanced to the left toward the cabin. "Be there, or we come looking for you. You'll be going against the vote."

There were a million excuses he could use to make the situation better. Every lie would've been easier to say than the truth. Rain wouldn't know if he was only returning Brandy's car keys or he'd forgotten one of his tools in her car or she'd asked him to check on her sticking door. But, he'd take responsibility for his actions. He'd fucked up. Big time.

He nodded. "I'll be there."

Club honor came first in his life. He'd broken a rule, and he'd take his punishment.

Rain left him alone. He walked over to his bike. Besides Rain, he'd been in the club more years than even Slade, the VP. A few times during his membership, he'd had to turn down the offer to stand at Rain's right side. It was nothing personal, because he respected his prez, his club, and his brothers. He preferred to distance himself, and not be disappointed.

Only Rain knew why he spent time in prison, but his president never asked for the truth. He'd spent seven years of his life shut away, five of those years as an adult in the worst penitentiary in Washington.

Positive there were more brothers in the club who'd spent time behind bars, he wasn't alone, but that was their business, not his. He'd told no one else about his past.

Tomorrow, he'd go in front of his club and let his family vote on his punishment. He rubbed the top of his chest, below his shoulder. Their judgment felt a lot like walking into a cell and hearing the door clang shut. His freedom was at risk for doing the crime of having sex with Brandy. This time, he was guilty.

"Fuck," he muttered.

He moved over to his bike, ripped his helmet from the Velcro strap on the bitch seat, and slapped it down on his head. At least he'd be the example of what would happen to any of the other members who tried to touch Brandy. He pushed the bike and flipped up the kickstand. Even that fact brought him no comfort.

"Wait," Brandy called, jogging across the parking lot.

Her shadowed form took shape the closer she came to him. Her black hoody hung down over her hips, covering a pair of black jeans. The Converse without laces on her feet showed him how important it was for her to talk with him, because she hadn't even taken the time to tie her shoes. Hell, the consequences of having sex with her couldn't even penetrate the lust he once again felt for her.

His stomach tightened and he forced himself not to react out of need to push her away. Rain already knew what he'd done. He couldn't change anything, but he wouldn't hurt her any more than he already did. She wasn't a bitch, she was a lady. A lady who needed a fucked up felon like she needed a gangbang.

And, even though he noted the significant differences between them—their age, their station in life, their personalities, he still wanted her.

She shoved her hands in the pouch of her sweatshirt, breathing hard, hair swept behind her shoulders but still mussed from when he'd ran his hands through it. He sighed heavily. Her bright, focused eyes tore him apart.

"I need to tell you something," she said, barely above a whisper.

He shook his head. "It was great sex, sunshine. That's all it was meant to be."

She was old enough to understand relationships started over dinner and wine, not on an old mattress inside a cabin, behind a biker bar. He moved his handlebars, holding his Harley up with his feet.

"I know." She nodded unequivocally. "Of course, I know that. I came out here so you'd understand that I have no delusions or…or thoughts that we'll repeat having sex. I knew exactly what I was doing, and what you were doing. But, you'd left like I'd contaminated you and—"

"No." He dropped his gaze to the gas tank on his bike. "Walking out of that cabin had nothing to do with you."

She tilted her head to the side. "O—kay. Fine. Great. I misunderstood then, and I can stop sounding ridiculous and leave you alone. Good night."

She backed up two steps and walked away with her shoulders back and her head held high. Maybe her strength and acceptance was the reason why he said, "Brandy?"

She turned around quickly. "Yeah?"

Emotions he tried hard to ignore surfaced, stealing his breath. He owed her the truth. "I broke club rules going into your cabin tonight and taking advantage of you. There's a meeting tomorrow, and you won't have to worry any longer. I'll pay for hurting you."

"But that's—"

"My fault. I broke club rules. I knew what I was doing and I'd do it again. That's why I'm sorry." He leaned forward and rested his forearms on the handlebars of his motorcycle. "Take care of yourself. Rain's a good guy. He'll make sure you're protected and your job is safe."

She took a step toward him and stopped. "I wanted to have sex with you and I'm not afraid to tell Rain what happened. We're both adults and it's not fair for anyone else to judge you for what you do on your own time. I'll talk to Rain and explain everything. He can't hold you accountable for a stupid club rule."

"The club makes rules for a reason and if I would've held up my end, you wouldn't be out here talking to me," he said.

She shook her head. "I don't agree, so I'll be the one to make everything right again for you."

His shoulders relaxed. What she said was probably the sweetest thing he'd ever heard someone say to him. "I'll handle Rain. You'll be fine and better off after tomorrow. Get some sleep."

She remained standing there, hands tucked into her hoody, eyes on him. He couldn't take anymore, and started his Harley. She continued watching him. He put his feet on the ground, pushed, and backed his bike out of his parking spot for club members only.

Brandy ran forward and put her hand on his arm, stopping him. "You're not an asshole," she spoke over the sound of the engine.

He grinned, because she was getting sweeter every minute. She was also naive and young. She had no idea.

"Go home." He lifted his chin motioning toward the cabin.

Her fingers tightened on his arm. "Thank you."

"For what?" he said.

Her mouth tightened into a thin line. He almost missed the slight shake of her head, refusing to answer. Then she threw her arms around his neck, squeezing him tight, freezing him in position, unsure of what to do, because everything changed when she held him.

He cleared his throat. "Sunshine?"

She leaned back dropped her arms, and walked away without knowing what he wanted to say. He stayed on his bike until she hopped up on the porch of the cabin and opened the door. Only when she was safe, tucked into her little cabin, did he ride away. Instead of cleaning up the mess he'd made, he'd created more questions than answers.

He'd seen the flash of pain flicker in her gaze when she'd told him thank you. He didn't do anything to deserve those words, so why was she thanking him? What would make a woman her age so damn understanding?

He'd treated her like one of the Bantorus bitches. From experience, he knew no one had taken away her choices during sex before. He'd forced her to let him do what he wanted, and she damn well got off on the power trip. Another man would've cherished such a willing participant, and showed her a good time. Hell, she almost seemed grateful to him and he hadn't done one damn thing special.

Chapter Seven

Brandy's plan to sleep the day away and ignore the world on her day off after a fitful night of worrying about Torque ended when the pre-paid cellphone rang. She grabbed the phone and answered after the first ring.

"Hello?" she said.

"Afternoon, baby," Radiant said, his tone upbeat as if he hadn't gone to sleep and still rode whatever drug high he was on from the night before. "Let's hear what kind of information my girl has for her new family."

Her stomach rolled. She'd never claim Los Li as her family. If she had a choice, she would never have gone to them asking for help. Her dad was her main concern.

"First, tell me about my dad? Is he okay?" she said, bunching the blanket to her middle to cover her naked body as if Radiant would be able to see her sleeping in the nude.

"Baby, baby, baby…" Radiant chuckled on an exhale. "I told you to trust me."

"Please, tell me if you've seen him," she said, leaning forward. "Does he seem…okay?"

What she wanted to know was if he was fighting and getting in trouble. When he'd come up missing, he'd left everything behind.

"He's fine," Radiant said. "Now, tell me what you've learned. I want every little detail, no matter how insignificant you believe it may be."

She pressed her hand to her forehead. "Uh, I heard Rain mention a ride in two weeks…twelve days from now, I guess. A man named Remmy is going, but I don't know who else."

Out of all the conversations she'd overheard between Rain and Bruce, Torque's name was the one that came up the most, but she purposely left out that information. She'd do anything to reunite with her dad, but talk was talk and not significant. For all she knew, Bantorus members hadn't chosen a team of riders for the job.

"What else?" Radiant said. "Think hard, baby. Use that pretty head of yours for something. We need more."

She closed her eyes and swallowed. God, she couldn't fail.

"I don't know anything else. I'm learning more of their names though. There's a big guy…Orca, but I don't know what he does for the club. Um, Pete, he's older and runs a garage here in Pitnam. Sh-Shift's Garage is the name. I tried to come up with an excuse to get the car you gave me into the garage to find out which Bantorus members worked there, but one of the members looked at the Cadillac in the parking lot instead. H-he questioned me about the car being owned by Los Li."

"What was his name?"

She clenched her teeth together, realizing her mistake. "It's…his name is Torque."

"All right, baby. Now we're getting somewhere." Radiant's voice lowered. "Tell me about Torque, and I'll see about you having a conversation with your daddy in the future."

"There's not much to say. He looked at the car, fixed some part—even though I didn't know anything was wrong with it. Then he gave me back my keys," she said, hoping that would be enough, and Radiant would understand that she didn't appreciate knowing she drove a car he'd used for Los Li business.

"So Torque's able to work now…"

She sucked in a breath, hoping Torque wasn't Radiant's target. "What do you mean?"

"Where's Torque during the day normally?"

"I-I don't know that." Her breath whooshed out and she hurried to continue. "They have a meeting today at three o'clock. I'm going to hang around inside the bar, even though it's my day off. I think all the members of Bantorus will be there."

"Good, baby." He paused. "It's almost time for that meeting, don't be late. You'll receive another call tonight. Make sure you answer, and I'll make sure your dad's near. If I approve of the information you bring me, you'll get to hear the old man's voice."

She threw off the blanket, afraid he'd hang up. "Please, can you—"

A click ended their conversation. She squeezed the cell in her hand, raised her arm—wanting to throw the stupid phone and yet knowing it was her lifeline to keeping her father alive, and muffled her scream of frustration. What did Radiant want from her?

She left the bed and paced the room. Nauseous and lightheaded, she walked out of the bedroom into the living area of the cabin and got a drink of water. After she'd soothed the burning pit in her stomach, she stared down into the sink.

Rain was the president. Slade was the VP. Torque, Remmy, Jedman, and Bruce seemed like they were in some kind of leadership role on equal footing with Slade and only listened to Rain. She'd met the prospects and other members like Orca, Pete, and Jimmy, who seemed to go to Torque and even Bruce for information as if they were lower in status within the club. She set her glass in the sink. That meant she had six bikers who would have information that Radiant wanted. But which biker was he interested in?

Torque's name had brought more excitement from Radiant on the phone. She braced her hands on the counter and let her chin fall to her chest. Even though she'd had sex with Torque, she knew absolutely nothing solid about him.

She assumed he worked at the garage too, since he fixed her car. He came in often during the day and night, only to disappear into Rain's office or talk to the other bikers. As of yet, she hadn't seen him visit the bitches cabin. The fingers on his left hand were bare, she'd doubled and tripled checked to make sure he wasn't married—although, Rain didn't wear a ring and he was very, very married.

She stomped her foot, frustrated with her lack of knowledge. *Think, think, think.*

Torque dominated conversations, had little use for chitchat, and couldn't give a care what other people thought of him, including her. He'd warned her off as if he had a motive to be a loner.

He wasn't all bad. She bit down on her lip, remembering how he'd made sure she found pleasure last night before he did. He definitely wasn't an asshole. When he'd left, he could've kept walking, but he explained how he'd screwed up.

She balled her hands and thumped the counter. She wasn't blameless like he claimed. Her goal here was to save her father, not screw a biker.

She had no idea the bikers were held to the rule of not having sex with an employee of Bantorus. Protection was one thing, and she liked knowing she was safe, but she was an adult and could decide who and when to have sex on her own without anyone's permission. Rain telling her she was protected while she worked for him was quite different than telling her she was banned from sleeping with a MC member.

Her heart raced, and she hurried back to the bedroom and grabbed the phone. She had to hurry.

In twenty minutes, the Bantorus meeting would start. She grabbed a pair of jeans, a Tee, and a pair of socks. She skipped the panties and bra to save time.

After she pulled on her boots, she swept her fingers through her hair, eliminating any tangles and leaving it wild. She swept mascara over her eyelashes, and called it good.

Viewing herself in the compact mirror from her purse, she looked like she'd participated in an orgy. She shoved the makeup away. It was her day off. That's all she could do without being late for the meeting.

She left the cabin and walked over to the bar, entering through the backdoor. Rain's door was open. She knocked on the wall before she peeked into view.

Rain looked up from his desk, deadpanned her, and said, "Yeah?"

Oh, shit. She stepped into the room. "Can I talk to you for a minute?"

He motioned her to sit down. She closed the door, and then took the chair in front of his desk. Sitting on the edge of the seat, she had no idea where to begin.

"I think there's been a big misunderstanding." She nodded, gaining confidence. "You had told me I was protected after you hired me, and I'd assumed that meant nothing would happen to me while I was in the bar and living in the cabin behind Cactus Cove…from bar fights, robberies, and the occasional drunk who had wandering hands. Of course, I've never been around a motorcycle club and my only association with bikers was serving them drinks at my previous jobs in small groups…and in So Cal, where I worked, it wasn't a biker haven, so the ones who came in were different, not the kind of bikers you have here. I mean, they rode bikes like you guys, but they weren't—" She pointed at Rain's tats, his vest, and his boots he'd planted on the top edge of his desk. "Like you or the other Bantorus members."

God, she was rambling. She moistened her lips when Rain remained silent. "So, this protection thing…I didn't know it included making sure I never, uh, did anything with the guys. Not that I have any plans to jump in with the kind of women in the other cabin out back. I wouldn't do that, at all. Not that I think there's anything wrong with them or what they do or, um, don't do. I'm sure they're very nice and good at their job of being with the men. I'm not judging anyone or the men—"

"Brandy," Rain said, raising his hand.

She sat straighter. "Yes?"

"Can we get to the point?" he asked.

"I had sex with Torque. It's all my fault. I didn't understand I broke a rule or he wasn't supposed to…to do that with me. It was consensual. Really consensual." She clasped her hands together to keep them from shaking. "I don't think he should be punished for something that happened between two adults. I don't know how this works, but if it helps, I'll work overtime or on my day off today to pay his fine, or whatever his punishment will be. I also promise it'll never happen again. Swear on it. Not happening. Ever…"

Rain continued gazing at her, no hint of his thoughts showing in his eyes, though his mouth twitched, which seemed to be a reoccurring habit with him when they talked. Finally, he plunked his boots off the top of the desk and leaned his elbows on the surface. She flinched at the sudden movement followed by the *thunk.*

"I'll explain how it works." His mouth softened. "It's not your responsibility to protect Torque. He knows the rules, sweetheart."

"But he shouldn't get in trouble for something I wanted to happen," she said, losing hope of convincing Rain of anything that pertained to Bantorus rules.

"I don't care if you jumped him naked and manually inserted his dick inside you. A Bantorus never breaks the rules the club sets forth," he said.

"Okay, I get that part, but isn't there anything I can do to make up for my part in what happened?" she asked. "Torque can't take all the blame."

"Brandy…" Rain tightened his lips across his teeth. "Don't throw yourself down in the way of club business for Torque. He won't appreciate it."

"But—"

"Do you know his last name? Do you know anything about his past? Do you know if he's willing to commit himself to a relationship?" he asked softly.

She leaned back against the chair, verbally beaten, and shook her head. It wasn't wrong to share a moment with someone. Her head pounded, because it was more than a moment to her. He'd given her a gift no one had before. "He's not an asshole."

"I know that, sweetheart." Rain stood from his chair and walked around the desk.

She got to her feet and raised her chin. "Don't mention that I came here and asked you to go easy on him."

"Are you threatening me?" Rain's lips did their twitching thing again, and she realized he found amusement in the situation.

"Will you fire me if I say yes?"

He placed his hand on her shoulder. "No."

She shrugged his hand off and walked ahead of him to the door. With her hand on the door handle, she said, "I'd appreciate it if this was kept between you and me. Torque was there for me when I needed him…and he has no clue how much he helped, and I'd like to pay him back by not causing any more trouble for him."

"I'll keep this conversation private between us."

"Thank you." She opened the door and almost walked into Torque with his arm up, ready to knock.

Heat swarmed her neck. She gazed at him, taking in the way he studied her face, and the moment he realized why she'd come to Rain on her day off. His eyes warmed belying the hardness of his shoulders.

That mixed messaged further confused her. She wanted him still. They hadn't had time to explore each other the way she would've liked, and she had no idea his full name. Rain's questions had her overthinking the situation, but he was right. There was a lot she didn't understand, but she wanted to.

She knew Torque would never be happy spending more time with her. That was okay. She was here to do a job. Knowing him better was a bad idea anyway.

"Excuse me," she murmured as she squeezed past him and walked toward the counter in the bar.

She'd hang out, have a drink, and try to find out more for Radiant about the meeting. The best she could do is move on, and do her job.

Taylor switched places with Bruce behind the counter, so Bruce could go to the meeting. Brandy sat on the nearest stool, closest to the hallway, to keep an eye on who came and went to the back room. Failure soured her stomach, and her head began to ache in earnest. She'd wanted to help Torque, yet she feared Radiant wanted information only Torque could provide.

So, how was she going to make an excuse to stick by Torque if nobody would allow them to be together, and Torque wanted nothing to do with her?

God, she didn't want to be the one who handed Torque over to Los Li. He'd hate her more if he found out Los Li sent her here to do a job. Though he'd shown her consideration, attention, and at the end, he'd soften his reasons for walking away from her, she could tell he wasn't a man to mess with.

Chapter Eight

Rain motioned for Raul to shut the door to the room. Torque ignored everyone and took the second seat from his president's left beside Slade. He wanted to ask why Brandy was inside the office with Rain when he'd arrived, but the gavel hit the table, calling the start of the meeting.

The surprise on her face shocked him more than seeing her on her day off. Then her cheeks had turned pink and she'd looked away from him. He rubbed his thumb against his jean-covered thigh. It wasn't so much the awkwardness of the situation, but the knowledge that she couldn't face him.

She had an explosive personality that allowed her to go up against anything or anyone, especially him. Even last night before he'd left, she bravely faced him without speaking of regrets. While she worked, she kept all the men in line, while joining in the good-natured teasing and flirting.

If he was the cause of her lack of attitude and spirit, he wanted to make it right. If it were Rain who made her unhappy, he'd pay. Nobody, including him, had a right to steal Brandy's thunder.

"The next run is finalized. Remmy, Raul, Slade, Pete, and the prospect, Tim, will be riding down to meet Duck and his members from Lagsturns. This will be the last ride for Tim before we bring him up for vote. He's served eighteen months as a prospect, so keep that in mind." Rain gazed at Pete. "Are the cars ready?"

"All but that Mustang, which came with a lost title. We're going to the motor vehicle department today and getting that one put into my name," Pete said.

"No. I'll go with you and we'll transfer all six cars into my name. I want you and the garage off them in case something goes wrong, I don't want the business going down. That'll cover us for five cars, and I'll see if Susan can rush the new title through to pick up the sixth car before we're due to ride." Rain looked at Slade. "Since we're not driving the fleet of trucks we're using for transporting, make sure you pay the drivers ahead of time and give them a thousand dollar bonus to assure their cooperation."

"Got it," Slade said.

Torque watched the discussion. Usually he went on the runs. Though he turned down this one, he missed the action.

"Our end of the dealings with Lagsturns MC is legit, but that doesn't mean there isn't risk to involving ourselves with the Lagsturns. Since we merged with them nine months ago on a limited basis, they've stayed away as agreed. I'd like to keep that long-distance relationship going. That means we stay on guard until our riders are back. Every woman and kid stays in Pitnam. Agreed?"

A unanimous voting of *agreed* broke up business. Rain gazed at everyone, but Torque. "It's unfortunate that we have to have another voting today."

"Bring it," Slade said.

Rain thumped the table with his knuckles. "Torque fucked Brandy."

Torque held back the scowl and bullshit response he wanted to give at the dramatic flair of announcing he'd broken the rule. He lifted his brow instead and gazed at Rain, who'd turned and looked him in the eyes.

"As a club rule, we have two options. He can hand over his patch or pay the crime with two months' probation." Rain leaned back in his chair. "All vote to let Torque pick his punishment?"

"Nah," a chorus of votes said.

The outcome came as no surprise. Bantorus members lived and breathed club rules. There would be no special favors. It wasn't the first time he stood before the table and had his choices stripped away.

He was used to schooling his reaction. No one would ever know how the thought of losing his colors killed him. If he'd learned one thing in life, it was how anyone could rip away his freedom at any moment, without his consent.

"Aye if Torque should hand over his patch. All's final on unanimous votes," Rain said.

No one spoke or moved. Torque held his breath to hide the relief. Nobody was taking his patches. He'd take probation. It'd suck, but he'd deal.

"Aye if Torque goes immediately into probation…" Rain said.

"Aye," Raul added.

Slade and Remmy spoke their yes vote.

The bitter taste of judgment blocked him from any emotion. There was always someone ready to jump on him. First his father, then prison, and even after he was declared a free man. He was never truly free.

When it was time for the last vote, Pete said, "Nay."

Torque shifted in his chair. Votes only counted if unanimous. Without everyone's vote, Rain couldn't carry through with the punishment. *That* was something he wasn't expecting, or deserved.

"You've got the table, Pete," Rain said.

Pete crossed his arms over his vest-covered chest. "I can't in good conscious punish Torque for something my son-in-law did only two short months ago and wasn't punished for. Bruce went behind my back, the club's back, and disrespected himself and my daughter."

Torque's chest ached and he rolled his shoulders trying to find relief. Bruce had not only broken club rule, he slept with a member's daughter. It'd caused a riff in the club for a few weeks, until everyone—especially Pete—accepted that Bruce and Kristen were serious for each other.

"Brandy's an employee, not a daughter, an old lady, or sister. I believe if Torque takes this as a warning, we're good. If he believes there will be another incident between him and Brandy, he must notify Rain." Pete ran his forearm over his whiskered lower face. "It's the right thing to do."

"Aye if you agree, nay if you disagree," Rain said.

The vote came back from all members in agreement with Pete. Torque lifted his chin and met each of their gazes. "Understood."

"Meetings over." Rain chuckled when Raul swung his arm out and knocked Slade's stocking cap off. "Get the hell out of here and go work. Torque, you stay for a few minutes."

Pete stood, laid his hand on Torque's shoulder, and squeezed. He nodded his thanks.

The other members left after looking back at Torque, lifting their chins in acknowledgement that everything was cool between them, despite the ruling. Torque stood from his chair. He was ready to get out of the room. A half hour was about his limit in confined spaces, especially when he was the center of attention.

He remained silent, letting Rain decide when to talk. Now that he was free to seek out Brandy and find out what was going on with her, he had nothing more to say to Rain about what went on between him and Brandy.

The door clicked shut. Rain opened a bottle of whiskey, poured a shot, and motioned for Torque to take it. He downed it without taking a breath. Until the warmth hit his chest, loosening the tension in his fucked up shoulder, he hadn't realized how stressed he was about today's vote.

He held out the glass and let Rain refill it. Bantorus was his life. Living on the outside, he'd have a hell of a time finding a job. Nobody hired a known felon.

"Better?" Rain studied him.

He nodded. "Yeah."

"Good." Rain inhaled deeply. "We need to talk before you walk out that door."

"Vote's over." He shrugged. "I'd like to talk about the run we're making to California. I've changed my mind. If there's room, I'd like to go."

"Not this time. I need you here." Rain sat down and changed the subject. "You might as well tell me now if you have plans to fuck Brandy again. I don't need you knocking at my door, waking my woman and my daughter up at three in the morning."

The hit of alcohol to his system did nothing to soften the blow from the question. "Leave her out of this. Votes over, and anything between her and me is none of your business."

"It's a fair question. My newest employee walks into my office, gets her cute little body all bent out of shape over one of my members, and then my brothers refused to vote your ass out of the MC." Rain grinned. "It's been an exciting afternoon full of information."

He stared at Rain. "What did she say?"

"I made a deal with her, so I won't say." Rain lost the grin. "The person I worry about is you. I can't begin to assume you have feelings toward her, and because she's an employee I won't sit back and watch you hurt her."

He rubbed his shoulder. "Not trying to do that either. I don't know what the fuck is going on. She's…shit. Half the time, I don't think she's listening to a word I've said, not that we've talked much. She's got something going on in her head that I have no clue on."

Rain stood. "There's my answer. You're a free man, brother."

"What are you getting at?" He dropped his arm to his side.

"I've heard your side, and her side. You can do whatever the fuck you want on your own time with Brandy now that the club's had their vote." Rain walked to the door. "I need to go meet the guys at the motor vehicle department before it closes for the day."

He stepped past Rain and walked down the hall, his head spinning over what just happened. Somehow, Rain had jumped to his own conclusions, and the reasoning bypassed Torque's knowledge. He wanted to know what in the hell Brandy did to make a deal with Rain.

One step inside the bar, he spotted Brandy. Without missing a step, he walked right up to her, wrapped his hand around her upper arm, and led her across the bar. Halfway to the door, she balked.

"Stop." She jerked her arm, but he wasn't letting her go. "What are you doing?"

He stepped in front of her, lowered his head, and said, "I have questions and I can either ask them here in front of everyone, or outside where we can have some privacy."

"Fine." She pulled on her arm and he let her go. "We'll go outside."

She marched out the door ahead of him. He watched her ass sashay side-to-side feeling like a bigger asshole than normal, because he still wanted her despite the serious business that went down moments ago.

Chapter Nine

Several bikers hung around on the outer edge of the parking lot, while a few couples walked toward the bar, probably headed in to have dinner before the drinkers started coming into the bar. Brandy stopped on the sidewalk and turned around, ready to face Torque and get back inside before the other guys who were at the meeting left. She had to find out what happened and what they'd discussed behind closed doors.

She had to have enough information for Radiant when he called to be able to talk to her dad.

Torque appeared outside, his mouth set in a firm line. The crinkles at the corner of his eyes more pronounced, and his fingers curled into his palms. From the look of him, his punishment for having sex with her did not go over well.

He had the right to be angry with her.

She took two steps forward and said, "I can give you two hundred dollars. I know it's not much, but Rain pays me next week. If you need more, I can give the money to you then."

He rocked back a step and frowned. "What the hell are you talking about?"

"Your punishment," she said. "I'll help you pay off the fee."

He tilted his head. "You think because I slept with you, the MC will charge me a fine?"

"It's partly my fault. I could've said no." She clamped her bottom lip between her teeth.

"Sunshine…" He gazed up at the sky, shaking his head.

"What?"

He lowered his gaze and looked at her again. "It wasn't your fault."

"Takes two people to have sex," she said, unsure why he was arguing with her.

"Right." He stepped closer and his vest brushed her breasts.

Delicious shocks prickled her body and quickly warmed. She stared at the flames tattooed on his neck. "I'm sorry…about everything."

"Shut up," he said.

Her chin snapped up at his deep, gravely order. "I am sorry though."

"Open your mouth, sunshine." He lowered his head.

"Wha—"

He caught her lips in a kiss, sweeping his tongue against hers, sucking her in. Her body swayed against his. Instead of hardness, he kissed her long and slow, deeply, and possessively. Through several seconds she couldn't even count, he finally pulled back. She loved how he kissed her as if she belonged to him, as if no one could stop him, as if he wanted her. She marveled at the thought that she'd like to belong to him.

"You're going to get in trouble again," she whispered, unsteady and reeling from the kiss.

He rubbed his lips together, staring at her mouth. "I received the clubs permission to have sex with you."

She stared at him in disbelieve, not because he was a grown man and had to ask the club to have sex with her, but because he *asked* the club if he could have sex with her. The way he acted, it seemed as if he thought there was a chance of them repeating what got them in trouble in the first place. She'd bet her two hundred dollars on it.

"That's messed up," she said.

He framed her face with his hands, and lifted her chin until he could see in her face. "Yeah, so I want to know what you did to make that happen."

"Me?" She shook her head, but with his hands on her, she couldn't finish denying the members decision had anything to do with her. "I had nothing to do with them not punishing you."

"You made a deal with Rain," he said.

She went back through her conversation in Rain's office. The only thing she'd asked Rain to do was keep their conversation private from Torque. Obviously, Rain had kept his part of the deal.

"The only thing I did was offer to pay your fine for breaking the rules. Rain wouldn't let me. There was no deal," she said.

"You thought I'd have to pay money for sleeping with you?" he asked, his head getting closer as he talked. "Pay for having sex."

"Not with me. Because you had sex with me. Oh, nevermind. You know what I mean." She pushed away from him, needing space.

His closeness confused her. She swept her hair off her face and behind her shoulder, trying to get him off the subject of sex with her. He kept coming toward her. "I broke a rule. There are two options. I no longer can be a Bantorus member or—"

"What?" She lowered her hands to her side. "Did they kick you out?"

He shook his head. "Or, I'm on probation and away from the club for two months."

She closed her eyes a moment. "That's stupid. Where will you go?"

"I'm not on probation, sunshine." He held her upper arms and pulled her closer. "Pete went against the rest of the members. I'm only required to inform Rain if I plan on having sex with you again."

Her mouth opened, but no words came out. In a lifestyle where bikers had women living in a cabin, ready for anything that was required of them and God knew what kind of activities, Torque had to inform the club when he planned to have sex? With her?

"We're not going to have sex again," she said, backing away from his touch.

She continued walking, until the back of her boot hit the curb and then she turned around and headed to the door of the bar. He caught her before she could escape back inside.

"Hold on," he said, turning her around.

She shoved at him. "No, you hold on. This isn't a game. I work here. I live here. But that does not mean I'm going to be the subject of your meetings, now or in the future." She lowered her voice, practically hissing, "Especially having my sex life talked about and okayed by others."

"That's not—"

"My sex life is nobody's business but mine. Most of all, it's time every damn one of you stupid bikers learned that I'm not a bitch, including you."

She hurried through the door before he could stop her. Because it was her day off and she was mad, she ignored everyone in the bar and heading straight toward the hallway to talk to Rain in his office.

Except the locked office door stopped her. She knocked. When no one answered right away, she looked down the hall to see if Bruce was behind the counter. Somehow, she had to find out what happened in the meeting, besides the men dishing about her sex life. Radiant expected answers, and she was going to find them.

Torque entered the hallway, blocking her view into the bar. She glared, but he continued toward her until he'd backed her against the rear door of the building at the end of the hallway.

"I need to talk to Rain," she said.

"Rain's gone," he said, his hands roaming over her hips.

She froze when his fingers dug into the indention at her waist making her knees weak. Through whatever happened between her and Torque, she had to remember everything. "Where's he at?"

"DMV, getting things ready for a run." He lowered his mouth to her neck. "Today's your day off."

"So…" The muscles in her spine also weakened and her head tipped to the right, letting him access her neck. "I thought you were staying away from me."

"I am." He put his boot between her boots and pushed her leg to the side, widening her stance. "But not until after we have sex again."

Oh, wow. She closed her eyes. The firm, smooth tickle of his tongue on her skin mixed with his overbearingness was her undoing. Her mind went into overdrive, tallying all of the excuses why having sex with him was a bad idea. Then she crumbled every reason and tossed it over her shoulder.

Torque's hands cupped her ass, lifting her off the floor. She wound her arms around his neck, her legs around his waist, and planted her mouth on his. She rode his body as he walked. The destination unknown, she'd go with him anywhere as long as he never let go of her.

Too soon, he set her on her feet and broke away from her. "Keys?"

She dug in her pocket and handed him the ribbon she kept the cabin key on. His lips turned up at the corners and his eyes dropped to her mouth. She took a deep breath. His smile affected her in the most pleasurable way, and she had a feeling he didn't smile for just anyone.

He lived a hard life by codes and boundaries within the club, and yet still retained the wildness and freedom of a lifestyle that perplexed her. She let him take her hand and lead her into her cabin, into the bedroom, onto the bed.

It had crossed her mind more than once that Torque's change of attitude toward her hid more mystery than she could understand. Yet, she was here for her own purposes, and sex with Torque had nothing to do with her job she was here to do.

Torque sat on the bed and leaned back on his hands. "Strip, sunshine."

She stood before him and laughed, but the sound cut off at the way his eyes settled on her. His gaze was not on her body, but on her, straight into her eyes, and held her captive. Her breath came harsh and fast. Her heart raced. He ordered her to undress, but he was asking for much more. To shed her inhibitions and put herself out before him required trust.

He was a biker.

She was in trouble.

Neither of those things mattered.

Unable to deny him, she crossed her arms in front of her, lifted the bottom of her Tee, and pulled the material over her head. A shiver curled around the base of her neck, and she trembled. Vulnerable and needy, she turned her head.

"Look at me," he said.

She slowly let out the breath she was holding and turned her gaze back on him. He watched her while lifting his chin, his mouth softening in approval. He had all the confidence in the world, and she was tired, so tired, of being the one always in control, taking care of others, making sure the ones she loved were safe and happy.

"I'm right here," he whispered, never taking his gaze from hers. "Just you and me."

She swallowed, because the low, rough timber of his voice soothed her more than his words. As if unable to control her need to please him, she lifted her foot and planted her boot on the mattress between his legs.

Only then did he take his eyes off her and to her leg. The emotional reprieve brought heat to the surface of her skin. Nobody had ever concentrated on only her before. Not her parents, her coworkers, or the few friends she'd had over the years when she was younger. There was no hiding from him.

Torque pulled off her boot, and then her other boot. She shimmied out of her jeans, taking her socks off too. Before she could chicken out, she straightened glad she'd forgone her bra and panties earlier.

"There," she said, breathless. "I'm naked."

He sat with his shoulders slumped, his hands loose between his thighs and said, "I can see that, sunshine."

Because he continued to gaze into her eyes, ignoring her body, she held perfectly still. Unsure if he expected her to make the first move or he hoped she'd act like the bitches who hung all over the bikers, fondling, kissing, stripping, rubbing them, she waited.

"I'm not sure what you want me to do," she said.

Torque inhaled deeply and on an exhale said, "You're doing it."

Wow, he said the right thing. She relaxed and the moment she did, her whole body loosened and the wonderful sensations he always brought out in her returned. The apex of her thighs pulsated pleasantly and she wanted to reach up and squeeze her breasts to relieve the delicious ache building inside of her. But she couldn't take away this moment away from him.

He wanted her stripped and standing before him, and she wanted to give that to him.

He continued sitting there, content, and in no hurry. Yet his lack of moving forward baffled her. She lifted her foot to step toward him when he said, "For more years than I can remember, seems like fucking forever, I imagined a woman in front of me. She was naked. She could come and go if she wished. I thought of her as a representation of freedom. She willingly came to me, but when given the choice to leave, she stayed. She always stayed…"

By his tone, he seemed to be talking to himself but he was looking at her. She gave her head a shake, not understanding, knowing she was missing something important and what he was saying was about her.

"You stayed. I sent you away, but you came back and you stayed," he whispered, barely loud enough for her to hear.

She moved toward him then. His wonder and amazement swept through her, and she wanted to be the woman who never left him. She couldn't promise him tomorrow or infinity, but she could give him right now.

"I'll stay." She leaned toward him, cupping her hands around his face, and kissing him lightly, and said softer this time, "If you'll let me…"

He nodded under her touch. Her stomach fluttered over his quiet acceptance, and she stroked his cheek. His tenderness enthralled her as much as his toughness and bossiness aroused her.

He hooked her neck, bringing her forward, brushing his lips against hers. Then he let her go and stood. She changed places with him and sat on the bed, watching him unlace his boots and kick them off.

Unexpectedly, she understood him better in the last few minutes than all the other times put together. He was a good man. His warning to stay away from him came from something deep inside of him, a shield, a defense against hurting others. His behavior was one way to distance himself from others that she herself had used many times.

He had no idea how attractive she found him, because of that strength to go at life alone and on his own terms. She respected him more, because he had survived whatever put the haunted look in his eyes.

His belt undone, his fingers at the button of his jeans, he held her gaze. "Back on the mattress, sunshine."

She hurried to do his bidding when he shoved off his pants. He was ready, and she was willing. Once he rolled on a condom, he moved forward and put his knee on the bed between her legs. She scooted her body back farther on the mattress, widening her legs for him.

He stared down at her sex with hunger in his eyes. Her fingers curled, grabbing onto the bedspread. Her body vibrated in anticipation.

He lowered his mouth. With one caress of his tongue, her body became possessed. "Oh, my God…"

The bed rocked from her movements. She dug her heels into the bed, needing closer, reaching, and grasping.

He held her and there was something so perfect, so freaking fabulous in knowing he was taking care of her, she stopped struggling to reach her peak and let go, letting him take her all the way.

Her core wound tighter, hotter, more sensitive than ever, quickly spiraled, flooding her body. The pleasure culminated to her limbs, to the tips of her fingers. Almost giddy with relief, she laughed, sobbed, moaned, and screamed. Her thighs tightened against his head, holding him as she trembled through her orgasm.

She couldn't breathe.

She couldn't voluntarily move.

All she could do was soak in the comfort of having Torque cradle her in his hands, keeping her safe, and letting her rely on him completely. The powerful comfort was both unique and scarily too real. She never wanted to move.

Torque crawled up her body, wiped his mouth on his bare shoulder, and then gazed at her. Finally, he said, "We're not done by a long shot."

She stroked his face and nodded. "Your turn."

"No, our turn," he said, and she loved the sound of that.

He slid inside of her. Sensitive, aroused, and full of Torque, she gasped on an, "Oh, God."

Her body, once languid and satisfied, tingled awake. She raised her hands and grabbed on to his arms. Half afraid she'd die of pleasure, and half thrilled there was more to come.

"Hold on." He buried his face in her neck.

She wrapped her arms around him, swung her feet up higher and planted her heels on his tight ass. He bucked against her, and she moved with him. In, out, in, out, until she could no longer keep the pace. Torque lifted himself on straight arms. His chest expanded. She sprawled her hands on his chest, squeezing, clawing, and hurrying him. She wanted harder, faster, more.

There it was. She panted. Oh, God. Right there.

He pulled back and thrust once more. She catapulted into an orgasm. Clinging to him, she absorbed his climax. His muscles, hard as a freaking rock, pulsed against her. She quivered. Every little movement, even his breathing, stroked her, extending the pleasure.

He rolled to the side with her, and she inhaled a deep breath, laughing on a sigh. "Wow…"

Cradled in his arms, her leg flung loosely over his hip, she closed her eyes. She learned one more thing about Torque. The last time they were together wasn't a fluke of awesomeness. He was freaking awesome all the time.

Chapter Ten

Exhausted, unable to keep her eyes open, Brandy lay atop Torque's chest, her legs on either side of him, and her cheek resting in the crook of his neck. She never wanted to return to reality.

After he'd taken her higher than she'd ever been able to go with another person or herself, he'd taken her there again, and again. She yawned and the movement wore her out even more.

"You okay, sunshine?" he whispered, rubbing the length of her back.

She simply sighed happily.

His body quaked underneath her in silent laughter. She moved her arms, groaning in effort, and clamped her fingers onto his arm. "Don't. Move."

His body stilled. "Are you sore?"

The concern in his voice brought her head up. She groaned and attempted to smile. Even her facial muscles were semi-comatose. "No…absolutely no. Wore out and dead to the world. That's all."

He lifted his head and kissed her forehead. "Me too, but I need to get out of bed."

Disappointment had her rolling off him and sitting up. "You're leaving?"

"Not unless you want me too," he said, standing up and stretching his back.

The muscles across his shoulders bunched. She studied the tattoos covering his spine. The flamed tattoos she'd seen around his neck, also burned across most of his back, covering a hard body she still wanted to explore. She grabbed the blanket and covered herself. "No, you can stay. I'm not working until tomorrow night, so if you want to hang around…and talk."

He held his jeans in his hand. "Hang around and talk?"

"Yeah." She shrugged. "No pressure. I just thought if you'd like some company and seeing as how I'm not planning to do anything tonight, we could—nevermind. You probably have club stuff to do or have to work in the morning. No big deal. Maybe I'll walk up town and check Pitnam out. I hear there's a late night café open with Wi-Fi up on Main Street."

Torque dropped his jeans and strode toward her naked. She stood, wanting to meet him on an even playing field. Used to her independence, she hated the way she sounded desperate for him to stay.

He laid his hands on her shoulders, caressing her neck with his thumbs. "I'll stay for a while, okay?"

She nodded. "Cool."

His jaw twitched and his hands on her neck relaxed. "Cool, sunshine."

"Okay. Well, then. Um, I'm going to jump in the shower…make yourself at home." She scooted to the side, and he brought her back in front of him. "What?"

"You take a shower. I'll go grab us something to eat from the bar, and then if you want to talk, you can talk," he said.

Shit. Los Li. Her dad. Radiant would be calling. She pressed her hand to her forehead. "Okay, sounds like a plan."

She hurried into the bathroom, dropped the blanket, and stepped into the shower after the water warmed. For several minutes, she stood under the faucet letting the heat and water wash over her. They'd had sex—fabulous sex, but beyond their connection in bed, she had nothing to share with him, especially her private life.

She'd gone to Los Li for help, because she was desperate. She went along with the instructions to spy on Bantorus MC for Los Li, because she was desperate. No matter how hard she tried to convince herself she slept with Torque because she wanted to, she was afraid she'd made another desperate move that would turn out to be a huge mistake.

After washing her body and hair, she wrapped a towel around her, and hurried out to the bedroom. She wanted to have clothes on to keep her from thinking about sex with Torque. Not that the barrier would provide her with protection, but she had to slow things down and get back to the business of saving her dad.

When Torque spoke, looked, or breathed, she panted after him as if she could make her whole situation fade away. He couldn't help her. She also couldn't ignore the urgency to get Radiant the information he needed.

Desperate. She groaned as she grabbed her clothes out of the dresser. This was just a one—okay, two-night stand. They'd talk, they'd eat dinner, and they'd go their separate ways.

She yanked her Tee over her head, pulling her wet hair out from under the material. She'd keep things light and once dinner was over, she'd send Torque on his way before Radiant called.

She stepped into the legs of her cutoffs, and buttoned them. She'd use the time over dinner to discuss Torque's job, his relationship with Rain, and maybe Raul. Somehow, she'd find out more about the run that was scheduled. There had to be a connection she was missing between Bantorus and Los Li somewhere in this mess.

Twenty minutes later, she walked out into the main room of the cabin, make-up on, hair half dried, and fully dressed down. She even put her Converse sneakers on, because even her toes weren't safe from Torque's attention. She looked out the one window in the cabin. There were a few motorcycles parked in the lot, but from her location, she couldn't tell how many were out in the front parking lot. Maybe Torque decided to stay inside the bar or Rain sent him on a run.

If Radiant called now, she'd have nothing new to tell him. Besides the planned run she'd already informed him about, she couldn't even figure out what kind of business the MC did on a regular basis. Far as she could tell, the bar, the garage, and the hotel in town—which Rain owned all of them—employed mostly Bantorus members. They were also legit businesses.

There had to be something that she was failing to find. Los Li dealt in anything they could get their hands on to keep the Mexican mafia paying them. She shoved her fingers through her head and massaged her scalp, feeling a headache coming on. Her dad better not be mixed up with Los Li and doing something illegal.

The door opened, and Torque strolled into the cabin holding a cardboard box. Her head throbbed, and she realized she hadn't eaten since breakfast. She held out her arms and took the food from him.

"I don't have normal plates, but I do have paper plates," she said, setting the box on the counter. "I hope that's okay."

Torque approached her from behind, placed his hands on her hips, and kissed the side of her neck. "Not picky. We can eat out of the paper baskets. It's only burgers and fries."

"Men," she muttered. "We'll do paper plates."

Torque moved away and a chair scraped. Attuned to him in the same room, her hands shook as she divided the food.

"Why don't you have a man in your life?" Torque said.

She dropped the fries, spilling them on the plate. The talk was supposed to be about him, not her.

"I've only been in Pitnam for a little over a week. Most of that time learning the routine and stocking up on the essentials…like paper plates." She set his food in front of him and took the seat across from him at the mini dinette in the corner of the room. "Besides, I don't think I need a man at my side everywhere I go."

Torque finished chewing and leaned forward, planting his elbows on the table. "I get that you like your independence, but a woman like you needs a man to keep her safe."

He had no idea what she needed. She was still alive and able to sit here and share a late dinner with him.

"I have Bantorus MC protecting me." She popped a french fry into her mouth. "How many men are in the club? More than one, obviously."

"All counting, seventy two." Torque pointed his fry at her. "We have you covered."

For several minutes, they ate in silence. What should've been an awkward moment turned into fascination. Torque took eating seriously, and wasted no time finishing his food. She glanced at him again. While he ate, he looked around the cabin and kept his chair farther away from the table than needed. He moved constantly and he rarely lowered his gaze to look at his food.

His behavior was opposite of the attention he gave her while having sex. When he was with her, he focused on her.

She wadded up her paper napkin. "Do you have somewhere you need to go?"

"No." He stood and carried his garbage to the cardboard box he'd carried over from the bar.

She followed him to the counter, took a piece of Foil, and wrapped the other half of her sandwich, putting it in the fridge for tomorrow. When she was done, Torque had already moved into the living room and opened the door.

He then sat down on her couch. Confused, she sat beside him on the couch sideways facing him, and said, "Is it too hot in here?"

It was the end of September, and although the daytime temperature reached seventy degrees, the nights were rather cool.

He reached out and rubbed her bare leg. She shivered under the heat of his hand and reminded herself they were only spending the evening together talking.

"No. Are you cold?" he asked, his voice lowering a notch.

Needing to distract him from where he was going with the conversation in case it was his attempt to *warm* her up, she covered his hand, keeping him from wandering to another part of her body. "Just wondering why you opened the door."

"Your place is small," he mumbled.

Rain had given her one of the bigger cabins with a bedroom off the main room. The limited space never bothered her before. Though she once worked with a woman a few years ago who hated getting supplies out of the back storage room, because she was claustrophobic.

"So, you have to work tomorrow?" she asked, urging him to talk.

He nodded. "I have to go in early and pull an engine. Should be done by two o'clock or so."

"How long have you been a mechanic?"

His fingers flinched. "Probably longer than you've been alive."

She laughed, leaning over and nudging him with her shoulder. "Okay, let's get our age difference out in the open.

"You're twenty four, and I'm old." He leaned his head back on the couch, amusement in his voice.

"How did you find that out? I mean, how old I am."

He pulled her down, so she was laying with her head in his lap, staring up at him. She lay motionless, letting him smooth the hair away from her face. He traced the curve of her cheek with his finger, stopping to finger the diamond in her brow. She enjoyed the responsiveness from him more than she wanted to admit.

"Rain," he said. "He's talked."

She played with the edge of his vest. "I'm at a disadvantage. I know nothing about you."

"Not much to know." He traced her bottom lip with his finger. "Except this is the first time I've had a woman's head on my lap when her mouth hasn't been on my body, and instead she wants to talk."

She smiled. Secretly, she was like every other woman who wanted to stand out in a man's life and his observation made her happy.

"You thought I was a bitch when you first saw me," she reminded him.

"Always knew you weren't." He sighed and dropped his hand to his side. "I won't fuck you over and have you thinking there's going to be dinner and talking every night."

"Fine." She stayed on his lap. "Now you've got that off your chest and out in the open, you can relax. I have no plans to domesticate the biker."

"Sunshine, I don't—"

"I hear you. I do." She comically rolled her eyes and lifted her chin—which wasn't easy to do lying on her back on his lap. "Get this, *babe*. Tonight was great. The other night was great too, but I think tonight was even better than that night. Just being honest and maybe sex does improve with time and experience, I don't know…seeing as how I'm twenty-four years old and you're just plain old. Besides, you have some quirks that are making me freeze my ass off, like leaving the door open. I can handle that, especially when you say things like I'm the first woman who has put her head on your lap and talked to you. I like that a lot, just so you know, *babe*. If you ever do decide to come visit again, I'll probably not tell you to go to hell because for some reason, in my short, short life, I've never had a man focus all his attention on me before and I think it's all kinds of wonderful. That doesn't mean I'll let you use me or I'll try to ride on the back of your bike."

Torque stared down at her, his upper chest quaking, his warm eyes softened that the skin at the corners crinkled. All kinds of happiness filled her, and she grinned. This was the hint of the man she knew was inside of him and needed to come out more often. He could protest and claim he was a badass—and she believed him—but he was made to enjoy life too and somewhere or somehow, he'd forgotten how.

A half chuckle escaped before Torque clamped his lips together and smiled. "You've been hanging around the bikers too much. You're starting to sound like one of us with a talent for bull shitting."

"You think so?" She pushed into a sitting position, getting off his lap. "Honestly, it takes too much energy to shorten my sentences and grunt to keep my biker speech up longer than a minute."

He leaned toward her, hooked her neck, and brought her forward. He kissed her hard and deep, and then let her go. "I liked what you said. Though next time, maybe drop the *babe*."

"Oh, okay," she whispered, kissing him quick and escaping his hands. "You better get going, so you can get some sleep before you have to work in the morning."

"Yeah." He stood.

She walked him to the opened door. "It's been real, babe."

"Smartass," he said, before kissing her again. "See you—"

Her cell phone in the other room rang. She pushed away from him, backing up. "Sorry. I need to get this."

Not waiting for him to say goodbye, she turned and jogged to the bedroom. She dove on the bed, stretching to reach her phone on the nightstand and swyped the button. "Hello?"

"Close, baby. One more ring, and you'd be very disappointed," Radiant said.

She turned her head and looked into the hallway. Torque hadn't followed her. "Is he there?"

"First, give me the information."

God. She had nothing significant. "Bantorus had a meeting earlier and I tried to stick around to learn what was said, but Rain left immediately for—she pressed her hand against her forehead, trying to remember where Torque mentioned Rain had gone—uh, he went…"

"Brandy," Radiant said. "Think hard."

She stood and paced. "I am. I am. He went—I remember. He went to the motor vehicle department."

"Why?"

"I don't…he said Rain had to go there before the run they're making. I told you about the run," she said, her heart racing. "Can I please talk with my dad?"

"Who's he?" Radiant ignored her question.

"Who's he what?" she asked.

"Who told you Rain was going to the motor vehicle department?"

She exhaled. "Torque."

"Excellent." Radiant's voice became clearer. "Now, before I let you talk to your pop, remember, I'll be contacting you again. Keep your phone close."

"I will." She nodded, hugging her middle with one arm as silence came over the phone.

She strained to hear anything that'd let her know her dad was going to come on the line and willing Radiant not to hang up on her. The back of her neck prickled, and she paced to make the seconds shorter.

Finally, a familiar male voice bellowed, "Brandy?"

Her legs wobbled and she sank to the floor, the phone pressed to her ear. "Oh my God, Dad. Are you okay?"

"Where the hell are you?" her dad, David Haas, asked.

She rocked on her knees. "Pitnam, Washington. Where are you?"

"California, where the hell else would I be, honey?"

"Oh, God. Will you please leave Los Li and go back home?" she asked, fearing the worst.

"I can't. I need to make some money." Her dad lowered his voice. "I have a lot riding on this. Need to do right by you and work out a few things."

She stifled her anguish. He never listened. Half the time, she wondered if one of the past hits to his head hadn't given him brain damage. She couldn't understand his thirst to get into the predicaments he seemed to get into more frequently lately. However, the fact that he could discuss what he was doing was a good sign he'd listen to her. There'd been times when he'd shut her out completely and gotten himself in too deep.

"Dad, I need you to step back. This is important. Promise me you'll forget about everything, and not let anyone egg you into fighting," she said, knowing others were responsible for enabling his desires.

"Brandy, I need space," her dad said.

She pushed to her feet. "Can you describe where you are? Is it a room, a house, a hotel?"

"Hell, I don't know," he said.

Frustrated, she needed more information. "Be strong, Dad. Keep telling yourself that I love you. Brandy loves you. Keep saying it, and don't forget and go back home. I need you."

"I need—"

The phone disconnected. She screamed, "Dad."

She tossed the phone to the bed, and picked up the closet thing in reach, the lamp. She hurled it across the room, gasping on a sob. The base shattered, bringing her no relief. Her muscles spasmed, ached, clenched, screamed her uselessness to fix the situation. Her dad only had her to keep him safe. She couldn't fail again.

Chapter Eleven

A scream, followed by a low thud came from the cabin. Torque whirled around, jumped onto the porch, and opened Brandy's unlocked door. She was nowhere in sight.

"Brandy?" he called, walking straight to her room.

On her knees beside the bed, Brandy picked up pieces of broken glass. He strode across the room, picked her up, and sat her on the bed. "Do. Not. Move."

He walked out into the other room, grabbed the cardboard box he'd used to bring dinner to the cabin and found a broom leaning against the corner by the refrigerator. He returned to the room with both objects, looked at Brandy, dropped everything onto the floor, and kneeled down in front of her. Gone was the smile she wore earlier.

She stared at the floor, digging her nails into her palms. He pried her fingers away and held both of her hands to keep her from hurting herself.

"Hey…talk to me," he whispered.

She remained quiet, too quiet, and had no expression on her face. He glanced down to make sure she had shoes on, and then examined her hands, looking for any cuts. There were no marks or blood on her.

"Brandy?" He brought her hands to his mouth and kissed them. "Did you fall and break the lamp?"

She brought her eyes over to him and shook her head. He breathed easier. She was unhurt physically.

He tilted his head to keep eye contact with her. "It's only a lamp, sunshine."

"Yeah." She pulled her hands away.

He moved back to give her space, and she used the extra room to stand. He straightened, studying the room. The lamp would've been on the nightstand, and it broke on the other side of the room. It didn't get up and walk over there.

"Did you throw the lamp?" He stepped in front of her and brushed the wild hair off her cheek.

"I'll pay Rain back." She swallowed hard enough her throat muscles spasmed. "O-or I can replace it with another one."

"I'm not worried about the lamp." He held her face between his hands. "What's got you upset?"

"Nothing," she said.

He kissed her forehead. "Don't bullshit me, sunshine."

She refused to say any more. Heaviness settled over him and he let his chin fall to his chest. *Fuck.*

He'd thought having dinner with her after having sex would make things right. She deserved better than a 'Thanks for the lay' and him hightailing it out the door the way he normally did. She wasn't a bitch, and he'd treated her like one again.

"Do you understand what happened between us?" He brought her head up to look at her. "Do you?"

She frowned. "We had sex."

"Yeah, sunshine, we had sex." He brought her against his chest, holding her tightly, and said, "I told you from the start, I'm an asshole."

"Assholes don't apologize," she said without moving away from him.

He stroked her back, glad to hear her attitude returning. More than willing to let her believe there was something good inside of him to like and soften the effects of what he'd done to her, he said, "Sorry, sunshine."

Several seconds ticked by, and her hands came up and held on to his belt. His chest tightened. The power of one of her hugs was capable of sending him to his knees.

No one that he could remember ever hugged him, just for comfort. They always wanted something. Brandy wanted nothing. She expected nothing. She asked for nothing in return.

Because she never forced him to give her anything, he hugged her back because he wanted to.

"It wasn't you," she mumbled against his vest.

He absorbed that bit of information. If he hadn't angered her, and she wasn't upset about having sex—claimed she loved the sex—then what or who bothered her enough, she threw a lamp across the room?

He replayed everything they'd talked about, surprised to find most of the conversation centered on him, and he knew little about her. Everything was fine up until he'd closed the door. He leaned back without letting her go.

"Was it the phone call?" he asked.

"Huh?" She rubbed her cheek against him.

"Did the call you received when I was leaving upset you?" he asked.

She backed away. Her hand went to her throat. He stepped toward her again, and she shook her head. Someone had upset her, and he wanted to know who that person was.

"What the fuck, sunshine?"

"Please." She inhaled loudly. "Just go."

"The hell I will. Tell me why you were happy when I left and not thirty seconds out the door, I hear you scream and find you shaking and upset." He hooked her neck with his hand, pulling her closer and not letting her retreat.

She pushed against him, but he refused to give her space. Her whole body quivered against him, pissing him off more. "Who did this?"

"You wanted me to believe you're an asshole, well you're being an asshole now."

He let her go, opened her dresser, and pulled out at stack of clothes. Then he walked into the bathroom, found her toothbrush, her makeup bag, and her hairbrush. He returned to the bedroom and tossed everything on the bed.

"What are you doing?" she said, grabbing her phone and shoving it in her pocket before he could grab it.

He found her suitcase against the wall and threw it on the bed. "Pack."

"W-why?" she asked.

He paused a beat and started throwing her things inside the luggage bag when she refused to move. "Because I'm not leaving you here when you're acting upset, and I can't stay in your cabin to make sure you get your happy back."

"My happy…" She grabbed for her clothes, but he yanked her shirt out of her hands. "I work here, Torque. You can't do this."

"I'll make sure you get to work tomorrow night." He shoved the last of her things in and zipped the bag. "Come on."

"Dammit. I'm not going with you." She held out her hand. "I'm pissed off, not upset. Now give me my stuff back."

He grabbed her hand and pulled her through the cabin. At the door, he stopped. "Do you have your keys?"

She pressed her lips together and stared at him. He waited her out. Her chin lifted and she gave him the attitude he had no problems giving back. He pulled her out of the cabin, closed the door on a slam, and refused to back down. Stubbornness and thunder he could handle. Softness and tears left him useless.

At the backdoor of the bar, she threw herself against the door, stopping him from opening it. He growled his frustration. "You're not making this easier on yourself."

"Please, Torque. Let me have my bag and go back to the cabin. I'm fine." She held out her arms, raising his arm in the process, because he wasn't letting her go. "See?"

He grabbed the handle, kept the door open with the toe of his boot, picked up the suitcase, and hooked her waist with his other arm, carrying her inside the bar. In Rain's office, he set her down and closed the door, blocking her way.

She bore holes in him with a single look. Without taking his gaze off her, he spoke to Rain. "I've got my Harley outside. Can you take Brandy to my house in your truck?"

"Only have to ask once, brother." Rain came into view. "Everything okay?"

He kept looking at Brandy. "It will be."

Brandy snorted. "Rain, I'm not going to his house, and I seemed to have locked my cabin keys inside. Can I borrow an extra key?"

Torque moved around Brandy and put his hand on the doorknob. "I'll see you at the house in ten minutes."

"Give us twenty," Rain said.

He lifted his chin in acknowledgment and slipped out the door. Glad to put some distance between them to cool off, he headed straight for his motorcycle. He trusted Rain to make sure Brandy showed up on his doorstep. If she'd still been upset, he would never have left her, but since all she wanted to do is buck him every step of the way, Rain could probably get through to her better than he could.

Besides, Brandy wasn't his old lady, and he couldn't take her on the back of his bike. Club rules.

He pulled out of the parking lot, and headed home. Whatever made Brandy upset enough to throw a lamp—and he had good reason to believe that's what happened, he'd find out.

From what he'd assumed, she had no family around. He put more pressure on the throttle. Something about the way she'd fallen apart grabbed him and refused to let go. He never expected a woman as strong and independent to crumble, but he'd seen her face, he'd held her hands, he'd heard the fear in her breathing. He knew how it was to be scared. Nobody should go through that kind of hell alone.

Chapter Twelve

Brandy sat in Rain's truck next to a doll strapped into the middle of the bench seat. She looked at her boss to the doll to her boss. She was living a nightmare.

Rain put the key in the truck and glanced at her. "It's Lilly's toy. She'll only get in her car seat if her doll rides in the front."

"Strapped in?" She blinked in wonder at the big tough biker who would go to such a length to make his daughter happy. "Wow."

"Yeah...do anything for my girl." Rain's jaw relaxed and he let his hand drop from the steering wheel, letting the vehicle idle. "How much do you know about Torque?"

She looked out the front window and shrugged. "Enough."

Rain rolled down his window and leaned his arm out the door. "He's a loner. I guess every Bantorus member is to a point, but Torque…it goes deeper with him. I'd trust him with my life. That's why I have no problem delivering you to him."

She shook her head. "I'm your employee. I've told you I didn't want to go, and you escorted me to your truck, not even considering my wishes. You should have an employee handbook for all new employees. Because, really, kidnapping an employee should be on page one. Forcing an employee to do something she doesn't want to do will result in two weeks of vacation pay and two Friday nights off a month."

"Sweetheart, I'm not doing this for you." Rain shifted into first, eased off on the clutch, and drove out of the parking lot.

"Torque wants you, and I'd do anything to make sure he has you. I also wouldn't be handing you over to him if I thought he was going to cause you any harm, physically or mentally."

She slouched in the seat. "Well, that's encouraging. Except this doll strapped beside me has more of a say in what she does than I do."

Rain drove several miles through town and onto a back road without another word out of him. She was thankful for the silence. Since she'd received the phone call and Torque going ape shit on her, she hadn't had time to wrap her head around anything.

Her dad was in danger.

She had no idea where he was or how to help him.

If she said screw it on her job and left to go back home, she'd only have the option of walking right back into Los Li's clutches. Radiant would make her pay for failing. He'd either kill her, or give her to the gang members. She shuddered. She had to succeed for her dad and herself

Rain pulled into the driveway of a one-story ranch house. She scanned the area illuminated by the streetlights. There were several modest and clean houses around, but the one Rain parked in front of was the only one needing a paint job, the grass mowed, and the screen door lying in the overgrown shrubbery thrown away. She moistened her lips. Honestly, she wasn't sure Torque or anyone lived in the house. There was nothing on the outside that screamed occupied.

She turned to Rain. "Seriously? You're going to drop me off here and drive away even though I don't want to walk in there."

"Don't judge a man by the outside, sweetheart," he said.

Her mouth opened. Why were people always misunderstanding her? Bantorus members thought she was a bitch because of the way she dressed. She was twenty-four years old. Did they expect her to put on a sweater and long skirt?

"I'm not judging Torque or his house." She tapped down her anger. "I'm amazed that you of all people would make me do something I don't want to do. I don't want to spend the night with Torque."

"He was good enough that you had sex with him," he said.

"Oh, you did not just go there," She grabbed for the door handle, but Rain clamped his hand around her free wrist and stopped her. "What?"

"Don't hurt him," he said, softening his voice. "Give him time to understand you."

"I have no idea what you're talking about. This has nothing to do with him or me. He's just blowing this up into something it isn't. I broke a lamp." She stopped and inhaled deeply. "The lamp in my cabin, so I owe you for breaking it."

"Don't care about the lamp." Rain motioned with his chin toward the house. "Go to Torque. He needs you."

She glanced out the truck window at the front door of the house. Torque, hands in his pockets, stood in the opened doorway. She had thought Rain was lying to her about Torque needing her, but for some reason, just looking at him alone inside a house with no life, she wanted to go to him.

"I hate when other people are right," she muttered.

Rain chuckled. "I wouldn't expect Torque to pick a girl who wasn't smart."

She glared, but her anger diminished. "Don't let the looks fool you. I'm a badass behind the clothes and makeup."

He winked. "I'm sure you are."

She slid out of the truck, closed the door, opened the back door on the crew cab, grabbed her suitcase, and walked up the driveway. Torque remained at his spot in the house, and she stopped in front of him.

"One, it's never a good idea to order me to do anything. I'll fight with you even if I want to be with you tonight." She tossed her suitcase toward him. "Two, when I'm pissed off, you're only going to have to work harder at making me happy again, and I'm stubborn enough to make you pay for making me mad."

He glanced down, but not before she witnessed his lips curving.

"And three, *babe*…don't ever hand me over to Rain. If you've got a problem with me, then deal with me yourself." She stepped up to him, kissed his mouth. "You also need to mow your lawn so the neighbors stop talking about the badass biker dude down the road."

"How do you know they talk?" he said, moving over and letting her in the house.

She walked inside and turned around to face him. "Because I know people. You live in a nice, respectable neighborhood. You're a biker. That doesn't mean you have to let them continue believing you're not a good person when some of us know you are."

He closed the door. The lines on his forehead more pronounced and his cheeks above his whiskered face twitched with tension. "Who says I'm a good person."

She rolled her eyes, because the man protested too much. "Rain, Bruce, me…"

He huffed, picked up her suitcase, and walked past her. "I didn't have you come here to discuss me."

She ignored his comment and followed him through the kitchen to the living room, because she didn't come here to talk about her either. She gazed around his living space. A leather couch sat in front of the window. On the opposite side of the room, a mega huge flat screen television filled the wall. It was a guy's room, down to the motorcycle magazines thrown haphazardly on the end table and a bandana hanging off a nail pounded directly into the wall next to the hallway.

Torque walked into the attached kitchen. She moved over to the brick fireplace hearth and ran her hand along the cool bare surface. A woman hadn't touched this room. There were no plants, no Cosmo magazines, and no pictures. Women always displayed pictures.

She blinked the moisture from her vision. Even after her dad financially lost the bar he'd owned, including their apartment above the establishment, she'd decorated their rundown duplex with pictures of their past. God, she missed being home.

Torque touched her arm. "Drink?"

She accepted the glass he handed her, took a sip, and blew out her breath. Warmth rolled through her. "Thanks."

With his own glass, he parked himself on the sofa and patted his thigh. She sat beside him, and not on his lap like he suggested. Getting cozy and having make-up sex was not why she came over to his house. Actually, she had no idea why she was here and not back in her cabin, trying to straighten her situation around, except Torque and Rain forced her here.

He hooked his hand under her calf, scooted farther away from her, and brought her foot onto his lap. She pulled her leg, but he tightened his grip.

"What are you doing?" she asked as he pulled off her sneaker.

His hand caressed the top of her foot and he added pressure to the sole with his thumb. Her back stiffened and she almost came up off the couch. Then pleasure curled around her middle and she sank back against the couch cushion.

He continued manipulating her foot, massaging the areas that always grew tired at the end of the day from being on her feet all night at the bar. "Number three of your demands. Making up with you."

Okay, that was nice.

Pleasure radiated from his hands, through her foot, and straight to her heart. She studied him, knowing she should tell him it was all fluff. She wasn't serious, and yet when she'd told him off, she was telling the honest to God truth. He seemed to see through her attitude and picked out the important things she desired.

Torque was a dangerous man when it came to manipulating her to his good side. She had to concentrate on why she was working at Cactus Cove.

"That feels really good." She lifted her other foot. "But just so you know, we're not having sex tonight."

His hands never stopped moving. "You're sleeping in my bed."

"No. I'm not."

He dug his thumb into her arch. "No sex, but you're sleeping in my bed."

"I'll take the couch, and tomorrow I go back to the cabin," she said, determined to make a point he'd listen to and accept.

"My bed. No sex. I'll drop you off at the cabin before I go to work early in the morning." He moved his hands to her other foot. "In exchange for making me go without, you're going to tell me what happened during the phone call that took your happy away."

"I'm happy," she said, unable to keep the sarcasm out of her voice. "It's personal."

"I'm making it my personal." He dragged her foot closer. "I've had my cock inside of you multiple times and had you screaming my name. We're personal."

She refused to answer. He was entirely too familiar with her to bargain with, and she was too weak when it came to having sex with him to believe if he touched her, she wouldn't climb on top of him.

She needed a distraction. "Do you have family around? I mean, who aren't members of Bantorus."

His hands stopped moving and he pinned her with a look. She scraped her teeth over her bottom lip. Oh-kay. That was obviously a sore subject.

Accusations shone in his eyes before he covered himself by shaking his head. "Phone call, sunshine. Start talking."

She tried to pull her legs away from him, but he only tightened his grip. Life was so different here. Back home, she had no friends. She had co-workers, and before they lost the bar, she had employees. Not one single person ever asked her if they could help, or even inquired if she was okay.

Not that she'd let them, but Torque was different.

Torque demanded everything, while asking for nothing. His mixed messages confused her. However, she sat on his couch, in his house, within touching distance of him, and wanted to share her burden with him. She'd do anything to have that one special person to know what it was like for her to love her dad and only want to keep her world intact.

"I can protect you," he said softly. "I want to do that for you."

Somehow, he'd walked into her life when she least expected, offering her the world. She lifted her feet, put them back on the floor, and he let her. Maybe his compliance and stepping back to give her space helped her make up her mind. Or maybe she was desperate and lonely enough to take him up on his offer. Whatever the reason, she was tired, so tired, of failing.

Chapter Thirteen

Torque's request to come clean passed over Brandy's face, dulling her eyes and weakening her stubborn chin. Torque leaned forward, elbows to knees, and stayed quiet. He feared making matters worse, when all he was trying to do was help her.

The quieter she became, the more he wanted to kill the person who put the sadness in her eyes.

"Sunshine…I only want to help," he repeated.

"I'm sorry." She glanced at him and wrinkled her nose. "It's a long, confusing story and I'm ashamed of my failure to fix everything."

"I got time," he said, hoping she'd rely on him.

The last couple of weeks, she'd taken him to a place he never knew existed or that he wanted. He woke up every morning looking forward to pushing her away, and went home every night from the bar wishing he was going home with her. She'd sunk her claws into him and hung on when others knew to stay away.

She had him wanting to put some good inside of him, so she could find it.

He wanted to be that man she needed.

Hell, he didn't want anything bad to touch her, because he'd already made up his mind that she belonged to him.

"I will help, but you have to tell me what is going on," he said.

"My dad's the only relative I have," she blurted, rubbing her fingers over the palm of her hand in worry. "He's got some issues that require me to make sure he stays home, so I can keep an eye on him."

"What's wrong with him?" he asked, leaning back.

"He's crazy," she said as if stating the car she drove was a Cadillac.

"And you take care of him," he stated, respecting her more for her dedication to her father when roles should be reversed and her father was the one who should take care of her. She deserved someone looking out for her, loving her, supporting her.

"Yes and no." She moistened her lips. "When he's content, he's capable of working and looking out for himself. The problem is, he has something inside of him that is stronger than being a responsible man, a father, a...I don't know, a normal, rational person. That craziness overrules his commonsense. So, I make sure he stays out of trouble and doesn't ignore his responsibilities. When he gets the urge to go off on his own, I worry about him doing harm to himself or someone else. He makes bad decisions and can lose every penny to his name in a matter of hours doing stupid shit."

He rubbed his hand over his jaw, keeping his opinion to himself. Normal father and daughter dynamics were out of his comfort zone. He had no idea how families worked, except for those who were Bantorus members and married. He also hated to see her working and worrying over a grown man, even if he was her dad.

"I take it that was your dad on the phone earlier?" he asked.

She nodded. "Yes."

"But you're here, and he's…?"

"California," she said.

"Does he need money? Is it that the kind of trouble he's in?" Torque reached for her hand and held it between both of his. "I can help."

She sucked in air. "Don't do this," she whispered. "He's my responsibility."

"Sunshine, if it was one of my Bantorus brothers, I'd give everything I have to make sure they were safe and well. It's only money," he said, meaning it.

When he'd walked out from behind bars, nothing tied him down except Bantorus MC. He had a roof over his head, food in his gut, and a Harley to ride. Everything else was extra shit that meant nothing to him. He'd learned long ago that material things were useless when he had everything taken from him and the only thing that mattered was his freedom.

The way he saw it, Brandy's dad was stuck in his own prison without the ability of getting out on his own. Her dad owed his life to Brandy for being the kind of daughter who gave a damn, and someone needed to show her how much that meant to a person who literally was one day away from having his freedom stripped away.

Her hands shook. He raised his gaze and didn't like what he was seeing. Tears pooled in her eyes and her chin trembled. He was done for.

"Look at me." He waited until her attention came back to him. "I can't give you what most men can. I wish I could. Right now, I wish I were the man to bring you the happy back. I'm probably fucking this up by making you stay here, making you talk, making you hurt more, but I can't stop. And, I might not be able to give you what you deserve, but I can promise you that I will help you any way I can."

"Why?" she mouthed, no sound escaping her lips.

"I don't know," he muttered on a curse. "I've been places and done things that no woman should ever hear about. I need to protect you, and that includes protecting you against everything that's me."

"But you'll help?" she asked, leaning closer. "You'll give my dad money if that's what he needs?"

"In a heartbeat, sunshine. In a fucking heartbeat to get your happy back," he said.

She nodded, and kept nodding long after. Then she got up from the couch and paced in front of him. Her lips moved, and her gaze flittered around the room. He wanted to get up and go to her, but he held back. For how much he wanted to make the decision for her, she had to work out what was in her head on her own.

"This has nothing to do with money." She sat back down beside him. "I'm scared."

"Talk, sunshine," he said, leaning back and taking her with him. "You have my word. I'll protect you from anyone and anything."

She laid her head in the crook of his neck, her hand went to his stomach, and he absorbed the shakes he could still feel in her body. He swore to do whatever he could to erase her fears.

"Before I tell you what brought me to Pitnam, I want you to know how I got in the place I am. My mom committed suicide when I was sixteen. She suffered depression after taking care of my dad for years. I was the one who found her, because my dad had run off a few days before…he was chasing his own dreams even back then. Afterward, I don't know if he manifested his guilt over what happened, but when he's low, he's violent. I'm afraid he'll kill someone," she said, with no emotion as if everyone dealt with life crushing disasters every day."

"Jesus, sunshine, your mom—"

"It's okay. I'm okay. This is the only life I've known. It sucks when I really think about it, and I wish I could've saved my mom and knew what was happening, but I'm determined to save my dad," she said. "I need to stay strong for both of us, so let me be strong."

"Right." He closed his eyes, letting all the information she handed to him soak in. She never questioned his past, but trusted him. He could do the same for her.

She wound her arm around his middle, holding him tight. "Not long ago, we lost the bar my dad owned. The economy took a huge hit. The area we lived in had two other bars open up within three blocks and crippled our business, and we couldn't hold on. From there, my dad went on a rollercoaster of highs and lows. I tried to get him to agree to see a doctor, in case there was a medication that'd help him accept the changes in his life or calm him down—he's high strung, and he refused. I ended up finding work at a lounge on the other side of town to pay the bills, but that meant being away from him for long periods. Then one day, he disappeared. At first, I believed he'd come back in a day or two like he usually did, no worse for his absence, besides a black eye or broken finger from fighting. But, when four days went by, I knew something was wrong."

He opened his eyes, because she'd said her dad called her. That meant he was still alive.

"After two weeks, I was desperate to find him. I'd exhausted all the contacts he had, and had nowhere else to turn." She swallowed, and he felt the muscles in her body shift and the tension return. "Then one night a man showed up at the duplex and said he knew where my dad was and he'd take me to him. It turned out he's a really bad man. I'm scared of what he's going to do to my dad, to me…to you."

His arms tightened around her and he kissed the top of her head to keep from grabbing more ammo mags and riding out on his Harley after the mother fucker who had her running scared. "I don't need to hear the rest."

He understood so much more about her. Her dad was in trouble, she'd bailed him out, and somehow she ended up owing someone. Someone was blackmailing her—his gaze locked on to hers and he went back through everything that'd happened between them. The pressure in his head intensified as the pieces all came together, and he bit off, "Los Li."

One deep line between her brows appeared and she slowly nodded. "Yeah."

The shoulder Los Li ruined when they shot him twice spasmed, making him hurt all over again as if the injury was fresh instead of almost a year old. He ached to get up and walk the truth off. Her link to Los Li put him smack dab in the middle of protecting her and going to the club with the information.

"I need to tell you, so you can protect yourself." She scooted away from him and turned halfway on the couch to face him. "Los Li is using my dad, for what reason, I don't know. No doubt, they see him as a way to bring them money."

He sat forward and ran his hands through his hair. "And what are you doing here? Tell me you aren't coming after Bantorus. Do not tell me that."

"I can't," she said. "Radiant, that's the guy who came and took me to my dad—but he didn't. He blackmailed me into working at Cactus Cove and supplying him with information on Bantorus MC in return for freeing my dad. If I didn't come and work for Bantorus MC, Radiant was going to put me to work as 'a bitch' within Los Li in exchange to get my dad out of there. I'm not a bitch…"

"What the fuck?" He stood and walked over to the chair where he'd placed his cell phone.

Brandy jumped up and followed him. "Please, listen. Please."

"Give me a sec, sunshine," he bit off.

Fuck. Fuck. Fuck.

He looked away from her. She was working for Los Damn Li, and the fucking Mexican mafia. He rubbed his shoulder. The same motherfuckers who put two caps in him and walked away scotch free. No retaliation, no payback, no fucking nothing.

"Torque, I had—"

"Don't." He held up his hand and pointed straight at her. "Don't talk."

Fury deafened him. Los Li had made their way right into the core of the family, and none of them had suspected a thing. Already tense and jumpy, he wanted to ride out and retaliate. They'd used a woman who was alone, frightened to death for her father, and…

Brandy hugged her middle and waited silently for him to react. He should've known. He'd questioned her about the car she drove. He should've fucking known, but he was panting after Brandy and blind to what was happening around him with all the changes in Pitnam with Gladys retiring, and wasn't thinking.

He walked into the kitchen, opened the bottle of Motrin, and popped four pills in his mouth, not bothering with water. The pills barely made it down his constricted throat.

Most of all, he wanted to go after blood.

Brandy had no choice but to try to save her father, and walked right into a trap. She'd done the only thing possible. He braced his hands on the counter and let his head fall between his arms. He unknowingly took advantage of her, having no idea the turmoil in her life, and that fact settled on his shoulders weighing him down.

She was fighting to save the only family member she had left. Even while she struggled, she gave and gave more of herself to him than anyone had before. That point wasn't lost on him.

"Sunshine..." He pushed off the counter and turned around. "Come here."

She moved and stood directly in front of him, not touching, not stroking, and not leaning her warm body against him. He'd done this to her. She was afraid of being herself, afraid of the consequences, afraid of Bantorus. Afraid of him.

They might not know shit about each other, but he knew her. He knew the kind of person she wanted to be if given a half fucking second to live her own life.

Instead of waiting for her to wrap her arms around him, he stepped forward and embraced her. He cradled her head against his chest. It was time he gave to her, instead of taking.

"Tomorrow, we'll go, meet with Rain, and take the problem to the club," he said.

She stiffened. "No, Torque. He'll never understand."

"He has to know. I'll protect you, and I'll get your father away from Los Li, but you do not mention one more thing to Radiant," he said. "Swear to me."

She nodded against him. "I promise."

The situation worse than he ever imagined, he tried to figure out what Bantorus MC could do for her. All of the options brought danger to every single one of them, the town, and the club. He inhaled deeply. Los Li would pay. They'd pay for hurting his woman personally.

His chest tightened. *His woman?*

His loyalty had always been with Bantorus Motorcycle Club. Bantorus until death. The only time a woman came before club was if the woman was an old lady. There was no hesitation in what he had to do, because he wasn't going to walk away. Not this time. Not with Brandy.

"I should've known...," he whispered hoarsely, his throat closing. "I should've fucking protected you from the start."

He needed to safeguard her, and the only way he could do that was if she wore his stamp. Because he owed Bantorus MC for his freedom, he had to take the right steps and put everything on the table. That's the only way he could protect her.

He'd have the whole family behind her, but she had to know what she was getting into with him. She deserved to know the truth of who he was.

"*Babe*," she said, stroking his cheek bringing him back into focus. "It's not your fault. I should've told you before we got to this point, but I thought I could do what they asked of me and everything would be okay."

His heart squeezed, because her jack shit nickname in her big ass attitude and bravery, tore down walls he had no plans to break down.

"I can protect you." He filled his lungs and pushed through the desire to run out right now and head to California to pay back those sons of bitches for hurting her. "But there are a couple things you need to know about me before you make the decision to let me help, and you're not going to like what I tell you."

Her head titled to the side. "What?"

"I spent seven years in the state penitentiary for murder. I made connections inside, so when I got out, I hitched a ride to Pitnam where I walked into Rain's office—no money to my name, no bike, nothing but the clothes I had when they stripped me down. I pledged my loyalty to Bantorus MC, and that's never going to change. When I told you I'm an asshole, I meant it. My blood runs Bantorus, and I'm not giving you the choice of keeping this secret between us. But, I can guarantee you protection from the club, from Los Li, and provide you with everything you need to get your dad back and to never be scared again for the rest of your life, if you'll be my woman."

"No…" She shook her head.

"Listen." He placed his hands on each side of her face and forced her to look at him. "The only way I can protect you is by telling you the truth, and claiming you as my old lady. I know it's hard to hear and I don't blame you for what you're thinking. But, I'll do right by you."

"Claiming me?" she said.

"Before you get it in your head that this is temporary, it is not. You'll probably end up hating me many times before this is over, and sunshine, I'll make sure it works out because that's my job. That's what I have to offer you. You need protection. I can get that for you…if you're my woman."

"Why?" She shook her head. "I don't understand."

He braced. "Why did I kill—?"

"No." She pressed her hand to her chest. "Why are you willing to go against everything you've told me to now deciding to claim me as your woman?"

"Honestly?" He leaned forward until his forehead lay against hers. "I have no fucking clue, except you do something to my soul when I'm with you that makes me believe that I can share your happy, and I have a feeling that's the best damn feeling in the world for a guy like me."

"Oh, babe," she whispered, without a hint of insolence and only sweetness in her voice. "Y-you know I'm going to say okay, but it's not because I'm scared. You…you've given me something I had no idea I needed until I met you, and I can't imagine not having you in my life. Remember that, Torque, okay?"

He nodded. Her reasons didn't play into what was happening. All he understood was he could get used to her calling him babe in that soft voice and the tender way she touched him.

"Then, you're my old lady and we'll make it official in the morning. You've got my protection against Bantorus MC. I'll stand beside you."

"Thank you." She kissed him with the same softness he expected to get from her. "Okay, I am a little bit scared, but not because I'm with you."

Her confession pleased him. He couldn't say he was disappointed. In fact, he wanted to take her in the bedroom and show her exactly what he thought about their arrangement. He wasn't into love, but then again love had no place in his life. But there was no denying Brandy was his, and he'd make sure she remained his.

Chapter Fourteen

Torque placed the half helmet on Brandy's head and latched the strap. She moved her head around, surprised by the weight. Though the reasons behind why she was wearing a helmet seemed to be a huge deal to Torque, coupled with the last twenty-four hours with him had left her unbalanced and everything seemed foreign and awkward, including the dull black helmet.

"So, having me ride on the back of your bike is a way for you to tell everyone not to mess with me?" She pushed the hair off her cheek and tucked it inside the contraption.

"Yeah, something like that." He removed the leather bag on the back of his bike, uncovering a slim padded seat no wider than his hand.

"No way," she mumbled. "My ass is way bigger than that."

"You'll fit." He grinned for the first time this morning.

Last night, she'd fallen asleep with him lying beside her, holding her close. This morning, she woke up to find herself alone and Torque sitting out in the living room with the door wide open again. Afraid to question him on why he prefers to freeze, she'd closed the door and opened the window beside his chair a crack, before curling up on his lap. They'd both fell asleep for another hour of much needed sleep.

Torque shut the garage, and returned to the bike. "We need to talk before we head to the bar."

"Okay," she said.

"Rain and the other guys won't go easy on you, and there's a very good reason why." He looked off into the distance. "You'll need to let them have their say and ask their questions. There's a lot of bad blood between Bantorus members and Los Li. We have history with them and the Mexican mafia. Slade almost lost Taylor to Los Li. The scar on her face is a result of fighting for her life and surviving. Slade's not going to take the news well about what you've done by coming into the club and working against us. Raul thought Crystal was dead because of Los Li and mourned her before he discovered she was still alive and got her back. He too, will not like hearing what you've done."

"Oh, my God." She squeezed her eyes shut for a moment, blocking out the horrendous picture Torque created by telling her everything.

"The scars on my shoulder are from two bullet holes from Los Li over territorial rights. The second one almost put me six feet down. Los Li wants control over Pitman, and we won't give it to them," he said.

"Shit." She staggered back, but Torque brought her to him again. "I didn't know. I'm so sorry. God, they're going to hate me. You should hate me."

"Give them time to hear and accept the truth," he said. "I'll make Bantorus listen, and I'll talk until they do. Be prepared, because we're going to have a war on our hands. So, if you have anything you've left out or haven't told me, tell me now so we go into this meeting with all the details."

She shook her head. "I've told you everything. I only agreed to come here to save my dad. If I had turned down Radiant's offer to help me, I was under the impression that they'd kill my dad and turn me into a bitch for their gang. I had to do something fast, because I need to take care of him."

"Okay." He removed his gloves from his vest pocket. "Good enough for me."

She grabbed the front of his vest, stopping him from getting on the bike. "Did Los Li shooting you have anything to do with why you were in prison?"

"No. The shootings happened less than a year ago. I was in the wrong place at the wrong time." He rubbed his hand over his mouth. "Prison was a long time ago, sunshine. I was put away at sixteen years old, and then transferred to the state pen at eighteen years old to serve the rest of my time. I walked away a felon guilty of murder at the age of twenty three."

She held on to his vest. His nonchalant ease at stating the facts wasn't working for her. His actions belied everything he shrugged off. She didn't believe what he was telling her.

"You didn't murder anyone," she whispered.

His gaze snapped from her hand on him to her eyes. "You don't know me or what I'd do."

"I do." She tugged on his vest when he tried to step away. "I know we haven't known each other very long, but you're not guilty of killing someone."

"You'd lose that bet, sunshine," he murmured. "I'm guilty of many things, including taking someone's life."

It wasn't true. He was lying. He wouldn't meet her gaze.

She held on to him. "I'm talking about your time in prison. You were innocent."

He stepped closer and got in her face. Their helmets clashed. "What makes you so sure?"

"I just do," she whispered. "You might've killed someone before, but it was in self-defense or you had a very good reason. I don't believe you would never outright murder someone. A man that holds me and is giving up his whole life to take care of me when my world has turned upside down would not be guilty of murdering someone unless he was saving someone else. You warned me away, when you could've taken me without a second thought. You claimed me, to save me. I know it's not for love, but what kind of man does such a thing? I'll tell you. A man who believes in protecting the innocent. You know what it feels like to have nowhere to turn."

He kissed her hard. She accepted the tongue in her mouth, the crushing pressure on her lips, the heaving panting. There was no gentleness in the kiss. She fisted his vest in her hands and held on, while he shut her up and acknowledged she spoke the truth.

He didn't have to utter a word.

She believed in him.

She also lost her heart to him.

He pulled away, not letting her go. His voice broke when he finally said, "Nobody knows."

"What do you mean?" Her heart raced. "Nobody knows the truth?"

"No, not the club, and not even Rain knows the reason why I spent time in prison or who put me there. Seven fucking years, and that was only because the crime was done when I was a minor and they knocked eight years off my sentence." He held her tightly, and tilted his head back, gazing into the sky. "My father—he practically spit the word out—killed his business partner, placed the pistol under my seat in my Charger, and when the police questioned him, he led them straight toward me. I was ratted by my old man. My prints were all over the gun, because a week before, he'd taken me to the shooting range for some *good ol' boys* bonding time."

"Oh, my God. Did you tell them it was your dad?" she asked, her heart breaking for the young man who had so many years wasted and had to grow up before his time.

He scoffed and brought his eyes back to her. "No, because unlike my father, I don't rat. You have to realize my life was shit anyways before all this happened. I'd lost respect for my father long before he framed me."

"But you went to prison," she said. "He needs to pay."

"After the first year inside, I lived day to day plotting vengeance on my old man. It wasn't until I got out that I learned he died from bone cancer while I was behind bars. I can never get my years back or erase my past or make him pay. And, sunshine, what I've done since walking out of prison isn't going to get me citizen of the year. I've done things that would sicken you, and I'm leaving it at that. All you have to know is I'm Bantorus, heart and soul, and you will be protected."

She nodded, unable to think of anything to say. He kissed her once more, got on the motorcycle, tipped the bike up, and started the engine. She took his hand, climbed onto the skinny seat over the back wheel, and held on as he slowly cruised down his street.

In a matter of minutes, Torque pulled into the parking lot of Cactus Cove. Whether it was because he'd missed work this morning or she rode on the back of his Harley, a crowd grew around them before they came to a complete stop. She hopped off and scanned the horde. Every man wore a vest and a solemn expression. Many of them wouldn't meet her gaze, and she stepped over and slipped her fingers into Torque's hand.

He lifted his chin and motioned for them all to follow. As if marching in a parade and she was the only person in a chicken suit, she trailed behind Torque. It was one thing to confess all to Torque in the privacy of his own home, and another to come clean around a group of bikers who looked scary and possibly dangerous. The feelings were not much different from when she'd walked into Los Li's club and dealt with Radiant. Scarier than shit.

Torque poked his head inside Rain's office door. "Meeting."

Rain stood and followed Torque inside the room across the hallway. Then Torque stood beside the table, behind the chairs, while everyone filed in and took a seat around the table. She leaned against Torque, needing to know he was physically beside her. He squeezed her hand, and she held on tighter.

The door closed.

"Before Torque speaks, remember there's a lady in the room." Rain leaned back in his chair. "What's up?"

Torque looked around the table and returned his gaze to Rain. "I ask that you hear Brandy out, and know that I've claimed her as my woman. She's Bantorus. If anyone has a problem with that or me, I'll tear off my patches."

Rain's expression never changed. "All agree?"

The men voted unanimously in agreement. Brandy, lightheaded and sick to her stomach, stared at the middle of the table. Torque never told her he'd leave the club.

If word leaked out and the worst happened, Radiant would come for her. Her dad would be worse off, and now Torque would lose his family.

She turned into Torque and whispered, "I've changed my mind."

"Can't do it, sunshine." He kissed her forehead, turned her, and pressed his hand against her back. "I'm right here. Ain't going anywhere."

With Torque beside her and his hand claiming her, she started from the beginning and spilled every ugly detail about how she found herself working for Rain, under the Bantorus MC's protection. Her cheeks remained dry throughout her recalling of the events, but her throat burned and her head pounded. Halfway through, Bruce stood from the table, poured her a drink from the mini bar in the corner of the room and placed it in her hand. She lifted the glass and finished the rest. Afraid she was going to throw up, she put her arm around Torque and hung on to his vest.

"Proud of you, sunshine." Torque turned back to the members and said, "Since she claims Radiant's pressure on her eases when she mentions my name, I'm assuming he's after me. I want to know why he's after me. I was the lone vote to go after him months ago after I recovered…twice. Yet, we sat on it, and let Los Li win."

"We kept our territory," Rain said.

Jedman leaned forward. "Lagsturns MC updates have assured us that Los Li has stepped back. They're going through Idaho and around Pitnam to reach Seattle. From all evidence, it never appeared as if Torque was the target months ago when the bullshit went down with Taylor."

"Fuck this. What's this say about us when one of Los Li walks into our club, a woman, and jerks us all off," Slade said, standing to his feet.

Torque shifted and put Brandy at his hip, his body between her and Slade. "I understand where you're coming from, but remember, the woman you're talking about *is mine*. If you have a problem you can't get past, then I'll take off my colors."

Slade sat back down and looked toward their president. Brandy looked at Torque.

"I have a big fucking problem with this, amigo," Raul said. "Crystal went through hell running for her life."

"Damn right, and Taylor still doesn't sleep through the night. That's on my back. I'd kill each one of the sons of bitches," Slade said.

Remmy thumped the table with his fist. "Slow down. Is there an association between Torque and Los Li? The Los Li boys run the penal system from the inside. Torque's a felon."

"H-he's not a felon," Brandy said, frustrated over everyone talking over her head and not understanding what they were discussing.

The room grew quiet, all eyes on Brandy. She held on to Torque. "It's not true," she said softly. "It's not."

Torque's body had gone hard and she tugged on his arm. She whispered, even though everyone in the room was all ears, "Tell them the truth."

"They know the truth," he said.

Rain shook his head. "*I* know the truth, but the club doesn't know. It's not my business to talk."

"Well, fuck." Remmy pushed back in his chair, his eyes hard. "I think we need to know what the hell is going on."

Jedman adjusted his bandana. "Most of us have women, kids, that need to remain save. If Los Li's gunning for Torque, us, I'd like the whole story."

Rain said, "We've never held a member responsible for his past. Not one of you has had to share what brought you here. I won't require Torque to tell us what happened while he was up state."

"I agree." Bruce shrugged. "What matters is now."

Torque stepped away from the table, taking Brandy with him. Tension and doubts stunk up the room. Brandy turned her back on everyone and curled into Torque's embrace. She had no idea who was shaking the most, her from fear or Torque in anger.

Rain cleared his throat. "Before we get to how we're going to take care of this problem, we need to take the vote to the table. Everyone who wants Torque's patch removed say aye."

"Wait." She stepped away from Torque and directed her attention on Rain. "You can't do this. I won't let you decide his fate in the club when he did nothing wrong. He only found out last night that I was brought here by Los Li."

"Brother, get your woman out of here." Rain stood.

"No. You're judging him, Rain. Just yesterday, you were telling me not to judge. You trusted him with my care, and now you're throwing him under the bus." She leaned against the empty chair at the table. "If you want me to leave, I will. I'll go back and tell Los Li *you* fired me, and I can't get him any more information. I'll save my dad by myself. Do not vote on kicking Torque out of the motorcycle club, because of me."

"Torque…" Rain's voice remained firm, but his eyes softened. "Remove her, or I'll have someone else take her out of the room."

Torque wrapped his arm around her middle from behind. She squirmed, but he held on tight, walking her backward. She wanted to scream and throw something. What they were planning was unfair. Torque didn't deserve to have his life thrown away because she decided to trust him. If they wanted to get rid of someone, they could fire her.

Once out in the hall, Torque kicked the door shut and put her down. He kissed her hard, stealing her breath. Riled and scared, he still made her knees wobble. She pulled away, not ready to give up. Torque deserved to stay in Bantorus. He owed her nothing.

"Go back in there and talk with them," she said, placing her hand over his racing heart.

He kissed her once more, and said, "Club rules, sunshine. My freedom is in their hands."

The massive train wreck started with her. If she'd only kept her mouth shut. She clamped her lips together and muffled her aggravated scream. God, she hated Los Li. They took her dad, and now Bantorus was inside the room deciding on Torque's livelihood because of her.

"I need to do something, " she said. "I can't stand here and let them take what you love away from you. I never wanted this. I'd never do this to you."

Torque leaned against the wall, head bowed, feet and arms crossed, not hearing a word she was saying. Her heart broke for the man who was powerless to decide his fate. She'd put him in the position of choosing between her or the club. He'd never forgive her if Bantorus stripped him of his vest, his patches, and his family.

Chapter Fifteen

Not once during the years he belonged to Bantorus MC had he stood before the club and waited for an exile punishment to come down on him. Probation, yes. Reprimand, yes. But never a vote to take away his freedom. Blood roared in Torque's ears. The only thing keeping him from running out of the bar was the fact that he trusted whatever verdict they agreed on.

Fear still consumed him, because he'd gone through this before. Except this time was different from when he was sixteen and facing a jury. Back then, he had no one backing him. He raised his head, soaked in Brandy, and calmed. Brandy stood up for him, spoke out to his brothers, and believed in him. For the first time in his life, someone knew the real him that he never showed and for some fucking reason, she stayed. At his age, her faithful support was almost laughable, except it meant everything to him.

"Come here, sunshine," he said, holding out his hand.

She slipped her fingers into his palm. He squeezed. Yeah, it felt fucking great to have someone on his side and believing in him.

"I'm sorry." She kissed the back of his knuckles.

Without letting go of her hand, he wrapped his other arm around her neck, bringing her to him. Her warmth against the length of his body relaxed him even more. The extra energy came out of him in a chuckle.

"We'll survive," he said.

"Just like that, you're okay with whatever decision they make?"

He pressed his pelvis against her. "No matter what, you'll be in my bed every night. My cock will be inside you every day at least once or four times, and when I wake up, you'll be there with your happy, making my life a better place. I'd say I'm okay with that."

She lifted her chin, her eyes swimming with tears. "But your family..."

"Yeah." He swallowed hard. "I've trusted them the whole time I've been a member, and I'll go on trusting they'll do what's right for the club. Club comes first."

There were many times over the years, he'd backed up Rain, Jedman, Raul even though he was originally the president of Lagsturns MC, and Remmy, more times than he could count. He'd covered tracks, wiped records, and made the community of Pitnam clean and safe for everyone's family. Nothing would change because he claimed Brandy. He'd make her life safe and the Bantorus family safe the moment the meeting was over whether he wore the Bantorus patch or not.

A door slammed in the bar. He turned his gaze down the hallway, and shook his head in amusement at the trouble headed his way.

Crystal and Taylor marched toward him, purses swinging off their shoulders, high heels clicking on the tile floor, and both wearing determined expressions on their face. Raul and Slade's women were pissed, which wasn't an unfamiliar sight, unfortunately. Though he usually enjoyed their attitudes, because they were his brothers' women and he didn't have to deal with them.

Taylor ignored Brandy, who'd moved to his side when Slade's woman and lunged for Torque. He braced and caught her.

"I'm so pissed off." Taylor wrapped her arms around his neck. "But, congratulations."

"Thanks," he said.

Then Taylor stepped back and punched him in the gut. He *oofed* on a chuckle.

"It's not funny." Taylor fisted her hands on her hips and glared. "I just heard they're voting. As soon as I can get past that door, I'm going to tell every one of those assholes off."

"Sweetheart, let them be," he said, cupping Taylor's face and running his thumb over the scar on her face that she'd received from the ex Los Li member who'd dared try to take her life.

"You could've died saving my life," she said through clenched teeth. "Slade knows this. He owes you. I owe you. Kurt and Lee owe you."

Brandy stepped forward. "You saved her life?"

He shook his head. "No."

"Yes," Taylor and Crystal said.

Crystal leaned over and kissed Torque's cheek. "He also backed Raul when Los Li came after me. He helped keep me sane when I thought I'd lost Raul and never let me go unprotected."

"Holy shit," Brandy whispered, moving away.

Brandy walked halfway down the hallway, turned and marched back toward him. "I'm not the only woman who has had trouble with Los Li."

Torque, Crystal, and Taylor shook their head. He brought Brandy back to his side and tucked her under his arm. "I don't know how I'm standing out here keeping the Bantorus women entertained, but you all need to go do something else."

More clicking came from down the hall, and Torque spied Tori jogging down the hallway. He groaned. The guys inside had no idea that dealing with the women alone was punishment enough for him.

"I can't even talk right now, I'm so furious." Tori came to a stop and sucked in a breath. "Damn Rain, damn Slade, damn each one of those men. Are they drunk? How can they forget everything you've done for them? You've saved their asses, you're always the one they come to when they need help, and you've taken more runs then all of them combined, so they could stay in Pitnam with their families. You've even babysat Lilly, and Rain doesn't allow just anyone around our daughter."

Brandy's eyes widened. "You babysat?"

"It was the middle of the damn night. Lilly slept the whole time," he muttered.

He leaned his head back against the wall and blinked up at the ceiling. Hell, he hadn't done anything special. He survived and he was a Bantorus, just like all of them. The women were making shit up, and making him into someone special because they had nothing else to bitch about today.

The door of the meeting room opened. He brought his gaze to Brandy first and nodded, assuring her that whatever happened, nothing changed between them. She was still his woman, and he'd protect her. Kissing her softly, he told her to stay with the other women. Then he walked to the table with more confidence because when he'd stepped away from Brandy, he heard her whisper, 'Okay, babe' in her sweet and tender voice with no attitude.

As always, he looked at Rain. His president, one of the hardest men to read on a normal day, gave nothing away. "If you have nothing more to say, we'll go ahead and get to the vote."

Torque stood with his hands at his sides, his boots spread wide, his shoulders back. Brandy's acceptance gave him the confidence to move forward. He owed no one a story of his past. He wanted his brothers to accept him at face value, and he was self-assured that only then would he be truly satisfied with the outcome of the vote. "I'm good."

"Then sit your ass down in your chair. We have plans to make." Only then did Rain let himself smile. "You think any of these cocksuckers would let you remove your patches?"

Torque wasted no time. He sat and began the plan that would get Brandy free of Los Li, her father back in her life, and find out why the Mexican mafia wanted his ass dead.

Chapter Sixteen

For the next two weeks, Torque and Brandy kept up the charade of her working for Radiant while putting time in at Cactus Cove working. She moved in behind Torque at the pool table in the bar and leaned her body against him. Last night, the one phone call they were waiting for came. It'd been the longest weeks of her life, not hearing any news about her dad.

"Hey, sunshine." Torque continued his shot and then turned around.

She ran her hands up his chest, glad that the bar had closed and only Bantorus members remained inside. "What's the news?"

"I ride out tomorrow. We can't postpone delivering those cars any longer. Lagsturns won't wait without an explanation, and they're already nervous because we've put it off four days." He smoothed her frown. "We changed the riders around. Rain, Slade, Raul, Remmy, and I will be taking the load, and the second riders will drive the fleet."

"You think that's enough to bring Radiant out into the open?" she asked.

She'd given Radiant the information Bantorus fed her to try to set Los Li into a trap. Her mouth dried and she moistened her lips. Everyone voted for Torque drawing the danger toward him, and away from Pitnam and Brandy. She thought the idea sucked, but being a woman to a Bantorus member gave her no vote.

"I hope." He tilted his head. "You okay?"

"No." She kissed him. "Can we go home?"

Torque passed his cue stick to Jedman. Together, her and Torque walked out of the bar. She wanted to hide and keep him safe, but she was also hopeful the plan would work and Torque would find her dad.

Outside at three o'clock in the morning, only the parking lot lights lit up the gravel lot and there were too many shadows for her comfort. She shivered, wanting to run to the cabin and get inside. Finding out someone from Los Li shot Torque behind the bar and nearly killed him, she no longer felt safe on Bantorus land.

"Can't wait until this is over and we can go back to the house." Torque stepped onto the porch shielding her with his body, and unlocked the door.

She followed him into the cabin. Any future plans were on hold until she had her dad back and Torque safe again. "I find it strange that we had no connection until I set foot in Pitnam. The best thing in my life came from the worst thing to ever happen to me. How messed up is that?"

"One day at a time," he said, taking off his vest, folding it in half and laying it over the arm of the couch. "We'll deal with everything once this is over."

"Yeah, okay" She yawned. "I'm going to jump in the shower."

She left him in the living room. Too tired to do more than strip, wash, shampoo her hair, and quickly get out of the shower. The only thing getting her through the days at the bar were the other girls, since Torque wanted to keep his routine in case anyone watched the activity around the bar.

Taylor, Crystal, and even Ginger had her back during the day. She hated Torque working at the garage, even if he always had two riders with him. He was brave enough to think he could end Los Li coming after her by himself.

Wrapping her robe around her, she towel dried the drips from her hair and walked into the bedroom. Torque stood by the dresser naked. His body never failed to make her weak. Broad shoulders, muscled arms, and a stomach she couldn't quit touching. She tilted her head and smiled, warmed all over. God, he had a tight ass.

She tossed the towel in the corner of the room, bringing Torque around. She took in the front of him and moved toward him at the same time. He was beautiful, all hardness and badass. Her exhaustion turned to lazy lust.

His scars at his shoulder paled in comparison to the rest of him. She trailed her fingers over the roughened edges. Thinking about what he'd gone through ate away at her constantly. She was the one who was responsible for bringing Los Li back into his life.

The injuries still bothered him, even though he never complained. She'd see him rubbing his shoulder at the end of the day, and he always shrugged her concern off as him being tired from working at the garage. But she knew the truth.

"Let me take care of you, babe," she said, tilting her face.

A low growl came first, and then she was up in the air and tossed on the bed. Torque landed on her, bracing his weight. The pressure against her body brought a tremble of desire through her. Tonight, she wanted it all about him.

"Nuh uh," she said, pushing his arms until he rolled onto his back.

She moved with him, on her knees, and her hands on his chest. She glanced down, gave him a smile and the dreamy desire in his eyes had her crawling backward. Situated between his legs, she wrapped her hand around his hardness, putting her lips on him, taking him in her mouth, one slow inch at a time.

"Jesus," he half hissed, thrusting his pelvis off the bed.

The smooth hardness of his cock heated her tongue. She moaned, sucking and caressing him with each lick. Her sex throbbed in pleasure, enjoying having the control of taking care of her man.

She bobbed her head, which made her nipples brush against his thighs. She whimpered as the need to have him touching her became too much. Suddenly, he sat up and rolled her over onto her back.

"Want more of you, sunshine." He stretched across the bed, grabbed a condom from the nightstand, and handed it to her.

She tore the wrapper with shaky hands, because his mouth was on her breast. She arched up into his mouth. "Okay…"

He moved up her body until he kneeled on the bed in front of her. She lifted her upper half, and rolled the condom onto him.

She sprawled her hands on his ribs as he came down, and spread her thighs. As his mouth connected with hers, his cock slid into her wetness. He absorbed her moan, and she clung to him, taking his thrusts. Needing to move, she pushed and went with him as he rolled onto his back again and she straddled his cock, fully taking his length.

Skin to skin, she rode him. His eyes told her how much he enjoyed what she was doing. Rocking back and force, she rubbed against him. His hands captured her hips, helping her keep up the rhythm. She let her head fall back on her shoulder and closed her eyes. Only his harsh breath, the slapping of their bodies, and the sweet suction of her body holding onto him filled her senses.

"So fucking beautiful," he said, lifting her up and giving her height to plunge back down on him.

His cock touched something deep within her, firing her body, taking her breath. She begged and moaned. The act almost too close, too deliberate, too wonderful.

Then he lifted her again and put her back down hard, over and over. She leaned forward, and planted her hands on his chest, taking over the movement of her body with her legs. In, out, in, out, stroking him until her toes curled and her body screamed for release.

His grunts turned to a groan. The vibrations rocked through her. Her orgasm reached out and grasped onto her, stimulating her into one giant blast of pleasure. At the same time, he held her down, grinding himself between her legs, shuddering through his climax.

Delirious, still sensitive to the throbbing of his cock inside her, she lay down on his chest. Sated and relaxed, her limbs hung loosely around him, her sex pulsating in aftershocks every time his cock sighed in pleasure.

He wrapped one arm across her back possessively, holding her securely to him. She glowed in the aftermath.

Several minutes later, he whispered, "Sleep, sunshine. I'll protect you."

That's exactly what she did.

Sometime later, she woke up under the covers, alone in the bed. She sat up with a jolt. A light came from the main room of the cabin. She stood, wrapping the blanket around her, and walked out of the bedroom.

Torque sat on the couch, fully dressed down to his black boots, with the door wide open, staring out into the night. She never hesitated, but walked right to him and sat on his lap, covering them both with her blanket. Snuggled against his chest, she laid her head on his shoulder.

"Tell me why you never sleep all night in the bed and you like the door open," she said.

His arms went around her, shifting her body closer, holding her tight. After a while, she thought he wasn't going to answer when he finally began. "I had several different prison cells over the seven years I was locked up, and none of them had a window. All I wanted was to look outside and feel the breeze on my skin, to look farther away than ten feet. Every night—fuck, I hated the nights, I'd dream the walls were closing in on me."

She squeezed her eyes shut, not wanting to interrupt. He never talked about his time in prison, and she was afraid to ask and bring up the past he wanted so hard to forget.

"My one highlight of the day was the hour long period the guards would usher a group of us outside within the secured area." His chest rose and fell. "I loved the summer time and to feel the heat from the sunshine on my skin. That hour outside was the highlight of my day. For an hour, I felt alive, normal."

Sunshine. She turned her head and kissed his neck. "That's what you call me."

She felt him nod, and he said, "Best feeling in the world being with you, all day and night now."

Oh, wow. She snuggled closer. Her heart overflowed with wonderful. Others might call her crazy for finding love in the middle of her life falling apart, but she had no other word to describe how Torque made her feel. If what they had wasn't love, she didn't know what love was.

Chapter Seventeen

Three fleet haulers filled with cars ready to deliver to Lagsturns MC in California sat idling in the parking lot of Cactus Cove ready to go. Brandy stood on the sidewalk away from the motorcycles lined up and hugged her middle. Life had changed fast, but nothing could prepare her for the danger Torque and the other members of Bantorus MC were willing to take.

Her level of worry ranked as high as her worry over her dad. She loved her dad, but his choices had always been his own. Torque's choices came because of the kind of man he was, and she carried the blame. She'd never be able to live with herself if something happened to him, because of her.

She'd experienced the bad, the good, and the unobtainable with him. There were things about herself she had never known, and he taught her new things every day. Like, she craved his attention, not because his touch, his words, his time was hers. It was because she was better for having him in her life. She was happy with him. Somehow, they'd taken the impossible, and found a way that complimented both of them.

Now Torque was putting his life on the line to get her dad to safety and keep her out of the hands of Los Li.

"It'll be okay, honey," Taylor said, wrapping her arm around Brandy. "They've all been riding together for years, especially the first riders. They know what each other are going to do before it's done."

She nodded. "I wish I could help. This is my fault, and I should be with them at least."

Taylor squeezed her. "Welcome to lockdown. The best thing we can do is stay inside, so the men don't worry."

"I know, but if it came down to keeping Torque's life out of danger, I would agree to go back with Los Li to stop all of this. Maybe I should try to—"

Hands grabbed her arms and whirled her around. She shrieked, heart racing. Torque's face filled her vision, and she sagged in his arms.

"I swear, if you fucking step outside the bar while I'm gone, I'll beat your ass when I get back," Torque said, his face a rage of anger.

"Babe—"

"Don't babe me this time, Brandy," he said, shaking her shoulders.

The use of her name hurt. Used to having him call her sunshine, she wanted to take her statement back and erase what she'd said, but she couldn't. Today's run was too important, and he had to know there was still a choice on what they could do.

"I'm scared for you," she said.

His chin lowered and he inhaled deeply, gazing at her. "I know you are, but I've promised you I'm going to get your dad back for you if I can draw Los Li out."

"I know." She fisted his vest. "I'm scared of losing you. I should be the one getting my dad, not you."

He brought her to him, kissing her forehead. "Attitude and bitching with no commonsense. You fit in with all the other Bantorus old ladies."

"You're insulting me," she muttered.

He chuckled and looked down into her face. "Facts, sunshine."

Rain walked behind Torque and slapped him on the back. "Line up."

Torque kissed her, deep, possessive, and full of adrenaline. She moaned against his lips, overwhelmed. This was not the way she wanted to save her dad. Torque had no idea what he was riding into or how to deal with her father if he managed to find him.

He pulled back. "Stay inside. Bruce and Jedman will make sure you follow orders. Nobody will touch you."

"Okay." She nodded. "If you find—"

"I will find your dad," he stated.

"When you do, don't hurt him, okay? He's going to go crazy, and he could hurt you. Keep telling him Brandy loves him. Sometimes…sometimes that helps." She pressed her hand to her neck. "Call when you know anything, or even if you don't."

He moved backward away from her. "Go inside, sunshine."

Confidence rolled off him. She stood watching him walk away in his black leather riding chaps, full leather jacket—which were sleeves zipped into his vest, and his flame tattoos creeping up his neck. He pointed to the door. "Go now."

She turned and joined Taylor, Bruce, and Jedman as they surrounded her and led her inside.

Shut inside the bar under lock and watch, she sat at the nearest table and sank her head into her hands. Her stomach flipflopped and she continually swallowed the anxious feelings. Doubts crept into her head.

She should be concentrating on sending all the positive energy she could to Torque, to her dad, and yet inside, she had a hard time not mourning the loss of the two most important men in her life. She rubbed her hands over her face. She couldn't act like this. Torque would hate it if she gave up now, and she was not a quitter.

The riders left behind mingled at the counter of the bar in quiet tones, probably to keep their business from infecting the families present. Old ladies sat at the tables, holding babies, watching their older children play in the corner, and the teens played pool. The normal atmosphere she usually experienced on Friday and Saturday nights at the bar were absent. The solemn mood came out of respect for the first riders who were out on the run.

Across the room, Tori waved and walked toward Brandy. She mustered a brave front and put on a smile. Ever since Torque claimed her, the other women had gone out of their way to welcome her to the family. She still wasn't used to having others around to lean on, but she tried, for Torque's sake.

"Want some company?" Tori stood at her table.

Brandy scooted out the chair beside her. "Sure."

"I figured you were about ready to make a run to the back door, so I thought I'd try and talk you out of it. First lockdown is always hard, but it does get easier." Tori gazed over in the corner where her daughter was playing with some of the older children. "I think each of the old ladies has tried to break her way out of a lockdown at one time or another."

"Did any of them succeed?" she asked, wondering if she stood a shot at making it outside.

"Torque got shot in the last lockdown we had when Taylor went outside," Tori said, not pulling any punches.

The truth hit Brandy low in the stomach. She swallowed hard over the nausea that followed. Everyone praised Tori for her sweetness but right now, Brandy hated her for her cruel and unnecessary information.

"Twice," Tori added.

Brandy sat forward, curling in on herself. "Okay, I get your point. My ass isn't moving from this chair, now will you shut up, before I either punch you in the face or puke on your shiny little boots."

Tori smiled and patted her arm. "You'll do okay. Torque needs someone strong. You've got guts, girl."

"Yeah, well..." Brandy pressed her hand to her stomach. "I don't know whether to hate you or like you for how you stick up for Torque, so lay off what is happening outside the bar and distract me."

Tori laughed and quickly sobered. "What do you want to know?"

Where did she start? There were many things she was curious about and because her focus was on her troubles with Los Li and her dad, she hadn't asked.

She blurted, "Did Torque have something going on with Taylor before she got together with Slade?"

Tori's eyes widened. "No. Taylor and Slade were together when I parked my coffee shack in Pitnam. Nobody knew they were together, but they were."

"A secret relationship…wow." She searched for Taylor and found her by the pool table with a boy who resembled Slade in his proud posture and deadpan facial features. The lanky, cute, dark haired boy, about fifteen or sixteen years old, was taller than Taylor and much too serious, but one of those boys all teenage girls thought were bad news and crushed on hard. "Is that their son?"

Tori looked behind her. "That's Kyle. He's Slade's oldest son from his first wife. That boy's a serious heartbreaker. He has his mind set on running Bantorus when he's older and I doubt if he'll let anyone stop him. Rain already has him prospecting, even though he's way too young. Slade also has a younger son, Lee. He's the one making sure Lilly doesn't put any of the Legos in her mouth over at the kids' table. You'll hear a lot from him in the future, he never stops talking. Great kids, both of them, and even greater now that Taylor has showered them with the love they deserved."

New respect for Taylor formed within Brandy. She studied the way Taylor smoothed Kurt's hair out of his eyes and the way the boy indulged her while still keeping his coolness factor. It took a strong woman to raise another woman's kids.

Gladys weaved her curvy body past the tables and leaned down to hug Brandy. She smiled at the woman who she had replaced at Cactus Cove. "How are you enjoying retirement?"

"It sucks. I've got too much time on my hands, and not enough people around to boss," Gladys said, slapping Orca who walked past with a lit cigarette. "Take the smoke to the back room, fat ass. We have kids in the building."

Orca snubbed the cigarette out between his fingers, pocketed the filter, and kissed Gladys's cheek. "Hey, sweet momma. I've missed your bitching."

"You have not." Gladys shook her head, but wore a grin, obviously loving being back with her boys.

The others wandered off. Brandy stared across the room, no longer seeing the people. The chatter, the clink of forks on plates, the squeal of children transported her to what was happening outside. With Pitnam bordering Oregon, the bikers were probably halfway to Portland. It'd take Bantorus MC two days to arrive in California and meet with the Lagsturns MC.

Then what?

What did it mean to draw Los Li out in the open?

How dangerous would the confrontation be if it happened?

What condition was her dad in?

Where would the riders get help from if everyone else stayed at Cactus Cove?

"Brandy!" Tori knocked on the table, grabbing her attention.

She raised her gaze. "Huh?"

"The men will be all right." Tori sighed and squeezed Brandy's hand. "They've gone on a lot of runs over the years. This is what they do. They take care of Pitnam and us. Try to get used to it now, because this won't be the last time Torque will have to leave you in the care of Bantorus. But, he *will* come back."

"Right," she murmured, wishing she could believe that.

Tori leaned back against her chair. "Do you want a drink to help you settle down?"

God, the thought of alcohol on her upset stomach only made things worse. She shook her head. "No, I'm—"

The phone in her pocket vibrated. She jumped out of the chair, scrambling to remove her cell, while frantically scanning the room for Bruce.

"Bruce," she yelled, as she pushed her way to the hallway. "Someone get Bruce, right now!"

Halfway down the hall after the second vibration, she slid her finger over the screen and answered out of breath. "Hello?"

"Baby, baby, baby," Radiant said. "What have I told you? I've given you two weeks. The last information fell through. They never arrived."

She plugged her other ear with her finger to hear the conversation better. "I know, I've got information but you haven't called. Rain and some of the other riders left a little bit ago on the run. They rolled out of here at eight o'clock. Th-they mentioned riding straight through on I-5, keeping to the main interstate to stay clear of trouble. I…shit, I can't remember."

She scrunched her face. It took everything she had not to yell at Radiant over the phone. All she had to do is feed him the information Torque gave her, and hope he took the bait.

"All right, baby," Radiant said. "You've done your job."

"Then I can come back and get my dad?" she said.

"I don't think so. You see, your dad's not working out the way I'd hoped." Radiant sighed and uh, uh, uh'd, over the phone. "It's over."

"What? What are you doing to him?" she screamed. "What have you done?"

There was no feeling in her body. No heartbeat, no breath from her lungs, no noise filtered through her ears. Her shoulder hit the wall. Her legs no longer supported her and she slid down the surface.

She closed her eyes. "My dad?" she said, or hoped she had said.

"You failed, baby," Radiant said.

She dropped the phone. *No.*

It wasn't true. He was lying. She had to take care of her dad. He needed to be with her, not Los Li. She'd promised herself that she wouldn't lose him too. What more could she do?

Hands settled on her shoulders. She peered up into Bruce's concerned eyes. She shook her head wildly. "No. I'm supposed to help him."

"Sweetheart, let me take you to the office," Bruce said, slipping his arms around her.

She let him pick her up. Another woman…Kristen. She remembered her. Bruce's old lady appeared by her side.

"Come on, honey, let's get you some quiet and a drink," Kristen said, wrapping her arm around Brandy's back.

"No." She stepped when they moved her. "No, no, no…"

Someone screamed. She covered her ears, but the sound kept coming. Awful wailing pierced the hallway. Louder and Louder, she couldn't make it stop.

Only when her throat burned and she couldn't swallow did she realize it was her screaming.

Chapter Eighteen

After eight and a half hours on the road, Bantorus MC rolled up to the opened Cyclone gate outside Lagsturns and drove the car haulers into the compound. Torque sat at the curb on his Harley watching the procession. His stiff legs protested every movement it took to get off the bike. He pushed through the discomfort and walked off the long ride to California.

Duck, the president of Lagsturns MC, and Big Joe, named after his size, walked out to the sidewalk to meet them. Torque looked behind him at Raul and found his brother at the corner of the block, backed turned, and respecting his boundaries. The bad blood between Raul, banished ex-president of Lagsturns, made it impossible for Raul to face his ex-brothers.

Rain shook hands, slapped backs, and Torque repeated the greeting. Everything was a formality. Neither MC wanted to mingle with the other, but respect came freely.

Bantorus MC depended on a successful run. The delivery of cars meant a bonus in his check, but all he cared about was gaining information.

He'd half-expected Los Li to show their faces before they'd arrived. He'd searched for any sign, but not once had he picked up the sense that they'd had a tail during the ride.

Torque walked behind Duck and Rain, and beside Slade and Remmy, into the secured parking lot that served as the entrance to Lagsturns club. The aroma of burning grease hit his nostrils, and he rubbed the gloves he held in his hand under his nose.

"What the hell is that?" he said, peering up at the old two-story building.

Slade grinned. "There's a Chinese place next door on the other side."

Jesus, the air stunk worse than prison where he put up with rancid body odor and piss. He stopped beside the first car hauler. He studied the area, surprised to find only a half dozen Lagsturns members outside watching the deal go down. Either the Lagsturns were getting sloppy with their protection or they had no fear of trouble coming. His stomach tightened. If Los Li attacked while they were here, they'd be cornered off.

Rain went on ahead with Duck to look over the vehicles. Torque leaned against the outside of the building, and kept an eye on the activity and movement around him. A half hour later, Duck and Rain headed toward him.

"Everything check out?" he asked.

Duck smiled. "Excellent stock."

"Good." There were no misgivings on what Lagsturns were going to do with the vehicles once they were out of Bantorus hands. Torque widened his stance. "You got a minute to talk about a group we have in common?"

Duck worked his lips over his teeth and finally said, "I've heard talk."

The other Bantorus men eased back and walked a few paces away to give Torque privacy in hopes that Duck would give him the information he needed. Hope filled him.

"Seems I'm the center of some attention Bantorus is receiving, and considering I don't like everyone's eyes on me, I'd like to know why I've got a mark on my back."

Duck motioned with his chin. Torque followed the Lagsturns president over to the side of the building. The others remained behind, but within seeing distance.

After Duck lit a cigarette, blew the smoke out of his nose, he lowered his voice. "Jimmy Chain ring a bell?"

Torque stopped himself from rocking back on his heels hearing the name of the little mother fucker who he served time with in prison. He hadn't given the mafia rat a second thought in the twenty years he'd been out from behind bars. While in prison, Jimmy was the mole. If you needed information, you went to Jimmy. In return, he racked points up and never let you forget about them. Serving double life in prison, there was no way Jimmy was getting out.

"Yeah, I know Jimmy," Torque said.

Duck nodded. "He's dead."

"Inside job?" Torque felt no loss. A number of people could've wanted him dead.

"That's the rumor, but before he found himself without any options on the inside, he spilled his guts on everyone who owed him markers like a little girl looking for one more daddy to treat her wrong." Duck kept the information coming. "Your name was mentioned."

His head whirled at the news, coming up blank. He'd never used Jimmy or asked him for anything. "For what?"

The end of the cigarette glowed red. Duck removed the smoke from his mouth, flicked off the coal, and pocketed the butt. "Don't know, but Los Li is dishing out paybacks in Jimmy's honor."

"Ah, fuck," he mumbled.

The situation was bigger than he'd thought. He wanted information on David Haas, and doing so put him right in front of Los Li with a fucking target on his forehead.

"Thanks, brother," he said.

Duck shook his head. "You didn't hear it from me, so keep your thanks to yourself. Lagsturns are on a smooth roll right now. We don't need trouble with the mafia."

He nodded in agreement. "One more thing. Ever hear of David Haas?"

"The crazy mother fucker from south Cali?" Duck raised his brows and stared at him.

Shit. What more could surprise him today? He waited, because if Duck was famous for being a hard ass, he was also well known for talking. He liked nothing more than knowing everybody's business and he kept his hands in everyone's pockets.

"Yeah, that's him." Torque guessed that they were talking about the same person.

"Crazy, man." Duck blew out his breath. "You don't want to mess with Haas. He's old school. Ran the Solitude Bar and was a one-man army to many and never wore a tat or patch for anyone. Nobody messed with him. Last I heard, he'd gone off the deep end after one to many fights underground and put a couple guys in the hospital sucking on air tubes after crushing their throats. Not many people hired him after that. He was too big—Duck grinned, shaking his head in amusement—of a liability."

"Who does he belong to?" Torque asked, curious after hearing more details about Brandy's dad for the first time.

"Nobody." Duck laughed low and rough. "You'd understand if you see him. He's fucked up, man. Lost his wife…maybe five, seven years ago and has never been the same. Everybody wants him, but he doesn't go with anyone. He has a daughter. Hell, she must be all grown up now. He swears to stay off the payroll for her. But, I tell you, man. I'd jump through fucking hoops to bring him on Lagsturns side…crazy fucker."

His vision of walking away with Brandy's father and reuniting him with his daughter went up in smoke. He clenched his teeth. What else had Brandy not told him about her dad?

She acted as if her father was useless and mentally half gone. He slapped Duck on the shoulder. "Thanks, man. I owe you."

Duck walked with him back to the others. "You find Haas, I'll make a deal with you. He's welcome here."

"I'll remember that," he said.

After the money exchanged, the next run set in stone, Torque retrieved Raul and sat on his Harley waiting for Rain and Slade to come out of the building. He pulled out his phone. Brandy had some talking to do.

"Everything go okay, *amigo*?" Raul slipped on his sunglasses.

"Yeah." He glanced over at his brother. "You look okay. It seems no Lagsturns member snuck around the back and popped your ass."

Raul chuckled. "It's a good day to be alive."

Torque studied him. On the outside, Raul accepted his place as a Bantorus, but everyone knew it wasn't easy deserting family and turning your back on the club that you gave your sweat and tears to over the years. "Duck's doing well. He's calmed lately. He said they've hit cruise control as a club, and want to keep rolling."

Raul's chin lowered. "Good to know."

They sat in silence. Torque pushed the button on his phone. A screen shot of Brandy lying on the couch with him doing a selfie stared back at him. In the picture, she grinned happily at the camera, and he was frowning. He remembered the night, because he'd protested about her taking his picture, but finally gave in when she whispered please. He'd do about anything to hear her voice when she got all soft and whispery.

He pushed Bruce's pre-pay number. His brother answered right away. "Hey, let me talk to Brandy."

"How far away are you?" Bruce asked.

He turned and glanced at the building. "Sitting on the fire, right now."

"Damn, man, you need to haul your ass back here." A door in the background shut. "Los Li phoned Brandy, called the whole thing off, left her stranded here thinking they were going to kill her dad."

Torque was already off his Harley and walking toward the gate. "When?"

"About six hours ago. The old ladies are with Brandy, but she took the news hard. Lost her cool, and Ginger had to slip her a pill to calm her down. She's sleeping right now. We're putting her under watch in the cabin with two guys on her. She's losing it, brother," Bruce said.

"Heading out now." He disconnected the call, and searched for the other Bantorus members. He spotted them outside the backdoor and whistled. "Let's roll!"

Remmy, Rain, Slade jogged toward him. Together they headed for their bikes. He filled them in as they put their helmets and gloves on. In familiar practice, they pulled away from the curb and lined up, two to a row, with Remmy as the end man.

He trusted the others to have his back on the trip, because Brandy consumed his thoughts. What the hell was going on?

His unease over his woman pushed his concerns of Los Li paying retribution toward him for Jimmy Chain to the back of his mind. Brandy's devotion toward her dad came across sincere, but from Duck's information, her dad could take care of himself and has for many years.

Chapter Nineteen

Twenty-two hours since Radiant called off Brandy's job, and she had no idea what was happening, if her dad was safe, if Torque was okay. She thrummed her fingernails on the table in her cabin. The only solution she'd come up with was to go back to Cali by herself to continue the search once she talked to Torque.

Hopefully, Los Li dumped her dad off on the streets, and she'd pick up his trail. Enough people knew him, she was better off going and asking questions at home than staying in Pitnam.

Nobody understood that sitting here doing nothing wasn't helping the situation. She stared at the food Bruce brought over a couple hours ago and she'd left untouched. She couldn't deal with Bantorus members eyeing her with pity any longer, and they'd let her out of lockdown.

Bruce and Jedman stood guard outside her cabin. She was grateful for the time alone.

The other Bantorus members didn't fill her need to have Torque back with her. Her appetite fled. Her contentment escaped her. All her rational thinking disappeared the second Radiant hung up on her. The only person she wanted was Torque.

Only he'd know what to do, and right now he was God knows where, doing God knows what, for her. No matter how many times he assured her it was his job to protect her, she knew differently. She blew out her breath, planted her elbow on the table, and propped her chin.

All her life, she'd depended on herself. Her dad repeated to her all the time how family takes care of family, and they must not fail again the way they had with her mom. That fear of failing was one of the reasons why she'd continued looking out for her dad when her mom died. She couldn't trust strangers because only she knew what had driven her dad to step back into the ring. The others only wanted to use her dad for his ability to fight in the ring.

She laid her hands flat on the table, sprawling her fingers, and inhaled. Once Torque came back to Pitnam, she'd hit the road and go back to California. She had no other choice. That's what she had to do.

She stood and retrieved her packed suitcase from the bedroom. A quick glance throughout the cabin, and she was sure she had everything with her. Hollow and numb, she couldn't allow herself to think of leaving Torque right now. She'd deal with that once she had her dad safe and back with her. If she thought of what she was leaving behind, she'd change her mind.

She also knew Torque would not let her leave. He was that kind of man. The kind of man she needed and wanted.

However, she wasn't delusional.

Once she walked away, he wasn't the type of man who'd run after her. Regrets would always lay heavy on her shoulders, but she'd survive. Not saving her mom, unable to save her dad yet, and bringing Los Li back into Torque and the Bantorus MC's life would always haunt her. Torque didn't deserve to live in fear.

She had to be strong.

She hated being strong.

The door of her cabin swung open. She turned, expecting Bruce, and found Torque filling the room. Her body urged her to run toward him, but she stayed where she was. He gazed at her intently, taking her all in. Her body betrayed her. She warmed under his attention and craved a moment to put her hands on him to make sure he was okay.

Lightheaded from not eating and the valiums Ginger kept forcing her to take, she swayed. He was alive.

That's all she every wanted. He was back safe with his club, and they'd support him. He'd survive.

His shoulders tensed, his stance braced, his mouth barely moved. She looked away, puckered her lips, and blew the hair out of her face in an attempt to hide her conflicted thoughts.

"Come here," he said.

She ignored his request. "H-how did the meeting with Lagsturns go?"

He closed the door for once and moved toward her. "Sunshine, look at me."

Stronger than she was feeling and more determined than she'd ever had to be, she brought her attention back to him. "Did you learn anything about my dad?"

"More than I knew before going to Lagsturns." He cupped her face. "What the hell is going on with you?"

"I-I failed. Radiant let me go without a word about my dad. I had no idea if you were in danger or even able to come back.

Now I'm stuck in lockdown in my cabin with no way to help anyone. It's not a good feeling," she said.

His thumb caressed her cheek. "I know, sunshine."

"I had no idea when you'd get here or what was happening. I don't like not knowing what is happening to people in my life. I don't enjoy being locked up with a group of people I barely know and told to calm down. I also don't like the whispers around me and when I ask questions, I'm told it's club business, like I should know not to ask because I'm only a woman. Shit, Torque, nobody will answer me, and I keep asking about you and if anyone has heard, and they just tell me that I'll know when they know." She blinked back the tears that threatened. "I need to go home."

Torque's head went back, but he continued to hold on to her. "You are home."

"I mean, back to California. I need to find my dad. I don't know what Radiant did to him," she said.

Torque's touch softened until she leaned her cheek into the palm of his hand. He was steady, hard, and here. All three things made it impossible for her to ignore her feelings.

"I'll take care of finding your dad, but you're staying right here," he said.

She shook her head and opened her mouth to argue with him when he kissed her. Like his personality, he consumed her. Firm lips, nudged her mouth open wider. His tongue dominated her ability to pull away. She leaned into him, letting him support her with only his hands framing her face. The kiss soothed her desperation, clear down to her toes.

Weak and submissive, she was in his arms and off the floor before she could think of protesting. Not that Torque gave her time to formulate a word to stop what was happening. Even if he did, she'd never deny herself what only he could give her.

He took her to the couch. She was naked in a matter of seconds, sprawled atop the cushions, his fingers toying between her legs, his mouth at her neck, and her hips bucking the air.

She shook with need from the two days without him. More than anything, she craved him taking ownership of her responsibilities. His forceful attitude gave her no wiggle room. She had to trust him and she did, except where her father was concerned. She couldn't hand that part of her life over to him, and he had to understand it had nothing to do with her love for him.

"Babe…please," she said, needing him to stop, wanting him to continue.

Afraid he'd continue to weaken her resolve to leave, she closed her eyes and tried not to think about him touching, talking, breathing. Around him, she almost believed her dreams weren't shattering around her.

His tongue swiped the tender skin under her ear. "Say you'll trust me."

She bit her lip, her hips arching in the air to the pressure of his fingers on her clit.

Denial stuck in her throat. She couldn't.

"Trust me," he stated, taking her earlobe into his mouth.

The warmth of his breath left goosebumps on her. She sucked in her bottom lip and bit down.

His finger slid inside of her, while his thumb continued stroking her.

She moaned.

"Trust me with your dad."

She shook her head, trying to move away from his mouth that continued to lavish her neck, making her lose control. Her back arched bringing her hips up. He slid his finger in farther, and touched the spot that made thinking obsolete.

"Stay with me and together we will find your dad," he murmured against her skin. "I promise."

Again with his finger, and again she cried out in pleasure.

He stayed inside of her, bending his finger, stroking her G-spot. "Trust me, sunshine."

"God!" She thrashed on the couch, losing the battle.

The rush of warmth disbursed clear through her. She panted and bucked.

"Let me take care of you and your dad," he continued.

She quivered, holding back the impossible. Because no matter how deep her love for her dad ran, her heart belonged to Torque. "Yes…"

With her compliance, she relaxed and her insides rolled, one delicious wave after another of pleasure, filling her completely.

Torque remained at her side, slowly stroking her through her climax and back down to earth, never leaving her. She finally opened her eyes to deal with what she'd volunteered herself to do when he stood and unzipped his jeans, pulled a condom from his wallet, and settled himself between her legs. He thrust into her as if to make sure she stayed with him. Her body, already sensitive, greedily took his hardness, sighing in anticipation of more.

She'd missed him.

She'd missed this.

She'd missed how she felt when with him.

Torque braced himself on the back of the couch, one arm beside her head, and gazed down at her while moving his cock in and out. She ran her hands over his chest, over his scars, over his tats.

She had no idea how she'd deal with loving and needing one man, and loving and needing her dad. The strength she needed to make both of them happy seemed impossible for her to find.

She laid her finger over his lips, and he sucked her finger into his mouth. The erotic feelings of his tongue against her skin had her climaxing again, taking him with her. He groaned as his pelvis jerked in unsteady rhythm, until he lost his strength and laid down, pulling her over, and laying her atop his chest, her leg flung over his thigh, her head in the crook of his neck.

"Missed you, sunshine," he said, kissing her forehead.

She grabbed on to his words and tucked them away deep inside. She only hoped he felt the same after they found her father.

Chapter Twenty

Brandy covered a yawn mid-sentence and tried to bolster enough energy out of the espresso Torque put in her hand. Amazingly, yesterday after Torque got home and they'd settled on her not leaving Pitnam alone, she'd fallen asleep on the couch and didn't wake up until twenty minutes ago to find the sun peeking over the coastal mountains.

Sometime during the night, she was subconsciously aware of rearranging her position to lay her head on Torque's lap as he sat with the door open. He'd dozed, but she swore the man never slept a full night in a prone position.

"Is it going to be okay with Rain if you take off with me for a couple weeks?" She sat down on the porch step beside Torque.

He drank from his own coffee cup. "Already talked to him. He wanted to send riders with us, but I talked him into us going alone. He's called off lockdown."

"You think you'll be safe?" she asked.

From what she understood, Los Li wanted Torque dead because of some miscommunication someone received from a man in prison. With a hit on his back, danger chased Torque no matter where he went. However, the idea of him being in California, closer to Los Li, scared her. It'd make him too easy to find.

"I think Radiant pulled everyone back off me, and that's why he called and told you the job was over. I made a couple calls this morning, and words getting around that Los Li got whiff of

Jimmy Chain ratting everyone out for his own vendetta. They've called off all the hits," he said.

"Why would he do that?" She leaned against Torque. "They're all criminals. They lie and kill, but they'll take someone's word as being the truth? Doesn't make sense to me."

"Not much makes sense when it comes to Los Li, sunshine," he said.

She drank the rest of her espresso. "So, we're going to leave for Cali tonight?"

"I want to travel with you after dark when there's less traffic. You're not used to riding yet, and it'll be safer." He removed his hand and stood. "I have a friend who's doing some digging and trying to find out if your dad's still with Los Li. It's a long shot, because I have my doubts that he can get any news about what is happening inside Los Li, but if they let your dad go, we'll hear about it before we arrive. That's all we got to work with right now."

She stood, stretched up on her toes, and kissed him. "Thanks, babe. It helps. A lot."

Shouting came from the side of Cactus Cove and Torque's body went stiff before Brandy found herself hustled back onto the porch. Motorcycle engines roared to life. The backdoor of the bar opened and Rain whistled.

Torque turned around, his body blocking Brandy's view. Her heart raced, not understanding what was going on, and she clung to the back of Torque's jeans.

"Everyone roll out. Drive-by at the garage. Lock 'er down," Rain yelled.

Torque waved him on. "I'll cover the bar. Take the others."

"Lock it down, brother," Rain said, running for his motorcycle.

Torque removed the pistol under the back of his belt. She hurried to keep up with him. "What's going on?"

"Shots have been fired over at Shift's Garage," he said, grabbing her hand and running to the next cabin. He kicked on the door. "Everyone out and inside the bar," he shouted.

While he banged on all of the eight cabin doors and made sure no one was inside, Brandy ran beside him. No longer tired, her adrenaline spiked making her jumpy.

In the last cabin, two girls, barely awake, stumbled and ran toward the back of the bar to get inside. Torque paused, and she tugged on his hand wanting to get inside.

"Hang on," he said.

She squeezed his fingers, unwilling to part from him. "What's wrong?"

"Listen." He cocked his head.

She tossed her hair behind her shoulders to hear better, but all she heard was her rapid heartbeat pounding against her chest. "I don't—"

"Sh." He stalked toward the corner of the bar, away from the back door.

He gave her a look she interpreted as 'stay behind him'. She pressed against his back, squeezed between a rock hard body and even harder brick building.

Traffic sounds grew louder. Torque spun and plastered her against the wall, yelling into her ear over the noise that continued to grow. "Go to the back door, stay by me, and don't stop running."

Car tires screeched, engines roared, and gunshots echoed around her. Half way to the door, she could no longer hear what Torque was yelling. Heavy weight took her off her feet and her knees dug into the gravel. She stretched her arms out in front of her to stop her face from hitting the ground. Panicked, the wind knocked out of her, she clawed out at the rocks, trying to move failing. Strange voices yelled around her, stilling her struggles.

"Stay still," Torque said against her ear.

Without moving, she tried to see what was going on. She had a clear view of the back parking lot, clear to the cabins. The shots were close, so whoever was out there must be right around the corner in front of the bar.

Two more shots rang out. She screamed before she could stop herself.

Torque kissed the side of her head. "It's okay, sunshine. They haven't spotted us."

"Who is it?" she whispered, all confidence of them getting inside the bar gone.

He shifted his weight, and brought his pistol up near her shoulder. "They're driving cages, so I'd bet money on Los Li."

"Oh, God." Her muscles seized. "M-my dad. I need to go see if he's with—"

"You're staying put." He shoved his pistol in her hand, wrapping her fingers around the warm steel, and then lifted his weight to the side of her. "The safety is off. It's cocked. You've got eight shots. You see anyone, you shoot, and you keep shooting until the gun clicks."

"No." She pushed the gun back at him, but he wouldn't take it. "Don't leave me here. Take the gun. We can get inside. They won't be able to come in, and then the other bikers will come back and chase them away."

His eyes softened. "My only concern is protecting you. Now go!"

She scrambled to her feet and ran. A gunshot pierced her hearing. The sound sent her stumbling and she fell against the wall. She glanced behind her and found a car, slowly rounding the corner. She whipped her gaze to Torque who stood at the corner between her and the car with a pistol in his hand. She had no time to wonder where the other gun came from.

"Torque!" She changed direction and ran toward him.

He stepped in front of her, aimed his pistol at the car, and waited. She skidded to a stop beside him, shaking so hard she feared dropping the pistol. The vehicle stopped twenty feet away from them. She zeroed in on the black tinted windows.

"Dammit. Do. Not. Move." Torque kept one hand behind him on her hip. "Stay behind me."

The backdoor of the car opened. Torque widened his stance. She couldn't point the gun, because he was right in front of her.

A large body rolled out of the car landing on the gravel with a familiar bellow. She dropped the gun in her hand and dashed forward. "Dad!"

"No." Torque stopped her, putting her back behind him. "He's got a—"

Bang.

Torque's body knocked into her, pushing her down. She cried out. Gravel dug into the palms of her hands, but the sight of Torque going down to his knees was what hurt her.

Before she could get to him, another shot came, even louder. She crawled, pushing Torque down and laying in front of him to protect him. "Oh, God. No, babe, no."

Blood seeped out of Torque's vest and ran down his neck. She laid her hands over his shoulder, trying to stop the bleeding. Her strong, badass man stared up at her, scaring her to death. The intensity in his gaze questioned her, but his lack of bossing her around told her this shit was real. She cried out for help.

The car behind her gunned its engine, sending gravel spitting at her back. She arched over Torque, protecting him from flying rocks when another gunshot went off. Torque's lower body flinched on impact. She screamed in horror, spotting her dad aiming in her and Torque's direction.

Pushing herself to her feet, she whirled around. "Stop shooting him. He needs help. Go get help."

"God damn, mother fuckers. Take their shit, and take their shit. Put a bullet up their ass, and their whores too." Her dad waved the gun around, pacing in the exact spot the car vacated. "Nobody, nobody screws me over."

"Dad!" She approached him. "Give. Me. The. Gun."

Her dad turned, tilted his head, and stretched his gun hand out to the side. "Messed up, honey. Messed up your momma. Messed up you. Messed up the bar, Messed up—"

"Dad, I love you." Brandy held her hands out in front of her. "I love you. Let me have the gun. I need to help Torque. Shit, you shot him, Dad. Stop, please, and help me save his life."

Her dad's attention shifted off her and he aimed toward her left. "That's it, dad. Nobody is going to touch you, but I need you to give me the gun and go get help."

"Protect you," her dad muttered.

Movement out of the corner of her eye had her jumping to the side, her worse nightmare coming true. She rushed toward Torque to stop him before her dad could shoot again, but he made it to her dad first. Both men went down in a tangle of arms, each fighting for the gun. Shocked Torque was fighting and not dying, she grabbed onto her father's shirt, attempting to hold him back.

"Don't, dad, don't," she yelled. "Let him go."

Nobody understood there was only one way to handle her father. Attacking him was not going to help. She had to get through to him.

Torque lifted his fist and punched her dad in the face. Blood squirted out of his nose and her dad's head hit the ground. She rushed to Torque. "Lay down, please. You're bleeding."

"I'm okay," he said, swaying to get up.

"Shit," she mumbled, grabbing him.

"Jesus..." He panted, falling back on his ass and letting his arms fall between his legs. "Son of a bitch."

Brandy hovered beside him, reaching out, but stopping before she touched his shoulder, his leg—that bled around the hole in his jeans—and his face. "You? How? You've been shot, babe."

"Flesh wounds." He groaned, leaning back. "Get my phone out of my pocket, hit Rain's number, and tell him to get his ass over here."

She followed the directions, keeping an eye on both Torque and her Dad. Before she pushed the button, she paused. "He's going to kill my dad."

Torque shifted his leg and grimaced. "He tried to kill me."

She swallowed. "I know, but…"

"Give me the phone." He held his breath as he strained to raise his arm. "I'll call Rain, and you stay away from your father."

"Torque, I need to get him somewhere safe and talk with him. He's not like this—"

"Give me the phone, sunshine, and step back," Torque said, struggling to his feet.

She did, because there was no way she'd ever be able to deny him anything or convince him to listen. Handing her dad over to Bantorus MC hurt almost as much as seeing Torque in pain. Guilt left her unable to know what to do. Her Dad shot Torque, twice.

This had to end. One way or another, she was going to end up hurting one or both of them.

Torque tapped the screen on the phone and then limped over and picked up the pistol lying by her dad's hand. She tried to help him, but he shrugged her away. She glanced at her dad, at Torque, her dad, and knew her and Torque's relationship would never work. No matter how much she loved him, she'd never be able to walk away from her father because of the damage he always left in his wake. Her dad needed her. Torque didn't.

Chapter Twenty One

Total chaos inside Cactus Cove came from two different directions. Torque sat in a chair letting Ginger clean and wrap his wounds, while he finished off the rest of the whiskey. The bellowing of outrage from Brandy's dad assaulted his ears, and the low murmurs between the Bantorus MC members had him wanting to join his brothers.

Unfortunately, the burning pain in his body meant he couldn't do anything until he stopped bleeding. At the first impact of the bullet, he'd waited for his life to end. Then he'd felt his arm, his leg, and all hell broke loose.

Because he couldn't do anything but sit while Ginger doctored his wounds, he concentrated on Brandy. During the whole attack, he'd witnessed her withdraw further into herself, and he didn't like it.

She'd walked right up to her father. All six foot six, four hundred pounds of muscle, holding a gun on his woman, was not a sight he wanted to see ever again. Even after everything congregated inside the bar, he'd watched her go between him and her dad. He wondered how long she'd had the darkness under her eyes.

Last night, she'd slept fitfully. He was used to running on little sleep, but his own bad night habits had kept her from resting. He should've let her sleep in, and held off their planned trip one more day.

Brandy walked back over to him and kneeled down on his right side. "I'm so sorry."

"I don't want to hear you apologize again. This isn't your fault." He hooked the back of her neck with his good arm and massaged the muscles. Her tense shoulders remained tight and unyielding. "You need to go lie down in the backroom until I'm finished here and rest."

"I can't." She drew back. "I need to take care of you, my dad, and…I need to talk to you."

"Get away from him," Brandy's father yelled, rising from the chair Rain had planted him in and ordered to stay. "You touch my daughter, and I'll kill you."

Jedman stepped forward, blocking Haas, but the Bantorus member only reached the man's shoulders. Torque spoke to Ginger. "Wrap it up, now."

He lifted his arm, allowing Ginger to tape the gauze that went around his shoulder and under his armpit. Once she finished and left him, he stood and headed in David Haas's direction.

"Torque, just let him spout. Once Rain's done with him and if I can take him away from here, I will." Brandy shifted sideways, walking with him. "He's mad, that's all. Once we're alone, I'll talk to him and calm him down."

He ignored Brandy's reasoning. He'd had enough out of the man.

"Sit down," Torque said, stopping a foot in front of Haas. "You're going to lay off Brandy now."

Haas stepped forward, his chest bumping Torque. Brandy gasped and tugged on her dad's arm. "Dad, stop…"

"Make me," Haas said, his chest puffing out, totally ignoring Brandy's request.

Torque refused to budge. "Shouldn't have done that, old man."

"Are you telling me what to do with my own daughter?" Haas asked.

Torque brought his head up, clipping Hass under the chin. Before Brandy's dad could react, Torque punched him in the diaphragm.

Hass landed in the chair hard, sucking air. Torque ignored the pain radiating throughout his body. "I'll only tell you this once. Brandy belongs to me now. While you were with Los Li, you lost any say in what she does with her life. That also means from right now, you act like a fucking man, so she doesn't have to make herself sick with worrying over your ugly ass."

"Brandy?" Haas's head came up and he looked at his daughter.

Torque continued before Brandy could say anything. "Respect, man."

"You're with this guy?" Haas ignored Torque. "I leave for—"

"You left, Dad. Again." Brandy sighed, and the sorrow written all over her face bothered Torque.

"Right now, you're going to shut up and give her space. You've done enough, don't do something that will make you lose her completely," Torque said.

Several beats went by and finally Haas dragged his gaze from Brandy to him, and he nodded without another word. Torque acknowledged his reply with his own chin lift. "Come on, sunshine."

He limped with Brandy over to a table, sat her down, and gingerly lowered his body in the chair beside her. "You wanted to talk."

Her gaze went from her father to him. "Rain's been more than gracious enough, after I explained the circumstances, to let my dad stay in the cabin with me for the next couple of weeks until I can calm him down and get him settled again. I can't have you staying with me. It'll only anger him. I need this time with my dad."

He looked over at the big man, sprawled in the chair. "He pointed a gun at you, sunshine."

"I know." She hung her head. "I know, but you have to understand, he wouldn't have shot me."

The throbbing in his shoulder intensified. "Jesus, Brandy. You were right beside me when he shot me. Luckily, his aim is bad, which proves my point. He could've shot you."

"Trust me. I'll be fine with him," she said.

"I have no problem letting him stay in the cabin by himself on Bantorus land. You can check on him during the day before you work, but after work, you sleep at my house. You need the rest, and I can make sure you get it," he said.

"I can't, babe," she whispered. "I can't."

Brandy stood and without meeting his eyes, turned away and walked back to her dad's side. Torque wanted to drag her back, but he could barely walk. The alcohol he'd downed before Ginger worked on his wounds already affected his thinking and his leg ached even when he didn't put his weight on it.

And, Brandy had made up her mind.

She'd had so little independence in her life, caring for her dad, and even running the business for the man. Torque wouldn't take away her freedom to choose between staying with her dad or making a life with him.

He caught Rain's eyes studying him. His President came toward him, and Torque held out his hand. Pulled out of the chair, he looped his uninjured arm over Rain's shoulders. "Get me the hell out of here."

Once outside, he said, "I want someone around her twenty-four/seven. Put one of the prospects in the cabin next to hers and have him sleep with his God damn window open. If he hears a sound from Brandy's cabin, he calls the emergency number for the club. I'll want everyone there if she needs help. I don't want anything to happen to her."

Rain opened up the passenger truck door. "Agreed."

He heaved himself up into the seat. "We need to get Haas medicated so Brandy can deal with her dad. He's wound up and wanting to fight. Does Sherman still deal on the side?"

The pharmacist across the border in Oregon often helped them out if they needed medical attention and couldn't chance going to the hospital and have their care documented. Torque took the seatbelt from Rain and buckled himself in.

"Already thought about that and put a call into Sherman. I also got Brandy's okay to do whatever we can for her dad. From the sound of it, he needs something to mellow out. He's a fighter with a lot of grief feeding into him that makes him angry. Once I drop you off, I'm meeting Sherman by the bridge. We'll get Haas started on something to calm him down and relax him." Rain shut the door, walked around the front of the truck, and got in the driver's seat.

Brandy was still trying to take care of her dad. He clenched his teeth together but whether it was the whiskey or the fact he was going home to an empty house, he said, "She's going to stick by her old man, and there's nothing I can do to make her realize he's not her responsibility."

Rain drove out of the parking lot. Torque let his head fall back on the headrest. His president let him have his quiet. Probably a good thing, because he wanted to punch someone. Fuck his shoulder. Even releasing his anger was impossible tonight.

"What's your take on Los Li?" Rain asked, turning off Main Street onto Cedar Street.

He rubbed his hand over his eyes. "If they planned to come after me, they had their opportunity to take me out today. Unless they expected Haas and his piss poor job of shooting me to finish the job for them."

Rain pulled into Torque's driveway and cut the engine. "I had a chance to talk to Brandy while the other members were getting Haas inside the building and you were getting the blood washed off you. She mentioned he's an ex fighter, stayed underground, and made a name for himself. Then after his wife died, he became uncontrollable, took chances and at his size, that made him a dangerous man to face. She claims he tells her when he's fighting, he can deal with life better—Brandy's words."

"Fucking great, and I'm expected to step back and trust that he has Brandy's best interest at heart?" he muttered. "The man's a giant. He's three times the size of Brandy, and I'm allowing her to stay with him."

Rain stared off at the garage. "He's also the man who held the baby Brandy in his arms when she was born, the one who probably taught her how to ride a bike, and wiped her tears when her first boyfriend broke her heart."

Torque's head spun. He glared at Rain. "Doesn't help. She's still my woman, my heart, my happy."

He slammed the truck door, knowing he sounded like a damn fool. Two agonizing steps later, he bit down on the discomfort and hurried to the house. By the time he reached the door, his head, shoulder, leg killed, and he wanted to puke. He unlocked his door and a thought came to him.

He whistled grabbing Rain's attention. After Rain rolled down his window, he said, "Get her a damn pre-pay and send me the number."

Rain waved and drove off. He hobbled to the couch and eased himself down. Uncomfortable in his own home, he stood back up and opened the door before finding his spot on the couch again. What Rain said about Brandy's dad raising her made sense, but that didn't mean he liked her being around him right now unprotected.

Though if he brought them both here, they'd be alone during the day when he worked, and he preferred having her close to the club when she wasn't working in case she needed anything. He closed his eyes. Hell, he rather stay in the cabin with her. They barely had any time to themselves between going on a run and dealing with Los Li.

Tomorrow, he'd talk with her.

The coolness of the night covered him. The open door, the breeze, the silence, it wasn't the same. He'd gotten used to having Brandy's warm body against him; her heartbeat to feel, her breathing to listen to, and the womanly curves to remind him he was alive. He shifted uncomfortably, unable to find a position on the couch to relax. He missed the soft sighs she gave him as she slipped into sleep. The way she'd smile against his lips when they kissed, letting him feel her happy, and the in-your-face-attitude when he tried to push her too hard. That same attitude he enjoyed also put the aloofness in her tonight, and she'd used the distance to create space between them.

And, he let her step away. He only hoped she understood he was doing it for her.

She'd had to be strong for too long. It was time she relied on someone else, and he wanted to be the man she leaned on. He wanted to protect and love her the way she deserved.

Hell, he missed the sunshine.

Chapter Twenty Two

Brandy's dad sat on the couch, staring at her as if she'd transported him to another world. She stood in the middle of the room; arms crossed, and challenged him to push her. Her stance was a familiar pattern she'd adapted a long time ago to deal with his sporadic moods and need to let off steam.

He in turn, had his arms crossed and had already pushed her to her limit. "You can't stop me from leaving."

They'd gone round and round all day after her dad woke up. At least one of them had slept, and it wasn't her.

"Try me," she said. "You've put me through hell the last month. I didn't know if you were dead or getting yourself in trouble. It ends now."

Her dad rubbed his hand over his jaw. "Honey, a man needs to enjoy life. You pamper me. I'm going soft. I'm getting old. I only have a few more years to get in the ring before someone takes me out."

She shook her head, not giving him an inch because if she did, he'd take off again looking for the excitement he used to find in the ring.

He *was* too old to fight. Any more knocks on the head and she'd lose him.

"You shot Torque," she said, swallowing her worry. "Twice."

He chuckled, shaking his head. "You know if I wanted that man dead, he'd be dead. He touched you. It's a small price to pay, and he's lucky I didn't drop the pistol and hit him with my fists. I should've taken him out anyway, after finding out what you've been doing with him. A biker? Honey, what the hell are you thinking?"

"It's my business what I'm doing." She glared, guilt piling up on her. "This is exactly why you're staying here. I'm working, and while I earn us enough money to go back home, you're staying put."

"The hell you say." He stood. "What happened to the money I had saved?"

"Besides the amount you took with you, I used what was left to pay the months' rent, so we wouldn't lose our only home while I looked for your stubborn ass."

Her dad sat back down with an *oomph*. "Damn, honey."

"Dad…" She walked over and sat beside him, sliding her hand into his big hammer of a fist. "Everything will work out. You just need to help me take care of you. I need you in my life, and going out and fighting, raising hell, and gambling is not the answer. I don't want anything to happen to you. Do you even realize how bad Los Li is and the danger I was in?"

Not to mention the danger he'd put Torque, Bantorus MC, and every woman and child in Pitnam in with his stupid move. Her eyes hurt, and she only wanted to close them for a few minutes and maybe this nightmare would go away.

"Boxing is all I know," he said. "Even before your mom…"

She squeezed his hand. "I know."

The loss of her mother broke her heart a long time ago, but continued to hurt when she watched her dad fight his demons. It wasn't his fault. It wasn't her fault. Her mother acted alone, no fault of her own, and though taking herself out of their life was selfish, as an adult, she realized everyone had choices.

Her father *chose* to fight in the ring.

She squeezed her eyes closed for an extra beat and sighed. Had she learned nothing?

She was making choices for her dad that weren't hers to make. He was an adult, and she no longer needed him to take care of her. In fact, it'd been years since she'd needed him to support her.

Until Torque, she'd never met a man who lived by an inner need to protect and live the lifestyle that made him happy. While Torque buried himself deep within the Bantorus MC, her dad had hung on to what he was skilled at, where he felt the happiest, and where his peers accepted him. It seemed that everyone wanted him to continue fighting in the ring, but her.

His behavior scared her. He was unpredictable. His grief and anger overtook his personal judgment. There were no doubts that he loved her with everything he had. He was a good father, a loving father, and a hothead.

God, she'd failed him and probably pushed him into the position he was in, because he had to hide what he loved to do from her. Exactly what she was doing with Torque, and she was miserable without him.

A knock on the front of the cabin broke up their talk. She stood, opened the door, and motioned Rain inside.

"Everything your dad needs is in the bag." Rain held up a brown paper sack.

She took the delivery from him and stepped back, wanting to ask how Torque was doing but knowing she couldn't while her dad was in the same room. "Dad…this is Rain Brookshire, my boss, and the president of Bantorus Motorcycle Club. He's brought you something to help you while you stay here with me and we can both get back on our feet."

Her dad pushed himself off the couch, crossed the room, and held out his hand. "Thanks for watching out for my daughter."

"I had help." Rain shook her father's hand, but cocked his head and didn't let go. "Seeing as how you shot one of my men, upset a woman in my employment, and put everyone's safety at risk by bringing Los Li to my town, I'll let you know that you mess up once, and we'll escort you out of town…without your daughter."

Her dad said, "You can't—"

"I can," Rain said.

Brandy glanced between the two men, holding her breath. Everyone respected Rain, but whoa…he was good. Her dad took Rain's threat and seemed to accept it with his silence.

"Torque owns her. You don't," Rain added.

Oh, shit. She crossed her arms and cupped her elbows.

Her dad's hand dropped from Rain's grasp, his shoulders widened, and the muscles in his jaw bulged. She stepped in between them and placed both her hands on her dad's chest. "Rain didn't mean that, Dad. Not the way you're thinking. He…They…it's a biker term. A code."

Her dad ignored her, and pointed his beefy arm over her head at Rain. "Explain yourself," he bellowed.

Rain picked up the bag she'd dropped, reached in, removed a joint, and offered the marijuana to her dad. She stared in shock.

"Are you kidding me?" she said, staring at the dope.

Her dad didn't smoke, he didn't do drugs. He was all about fitness and fighting. He just had a problem controlling his wanderlust and temper.

"It's legal in Washington." Rain's mouth twitched. "I think it's time for your dad and I to talk and you've got a job to do."

She wanted to stay and protect Rain. Her dad would annihilate him if he mentioned Torque claimed her, and she belonged to Bantorus MC now. Though, her dad wasn't dumb. Maybe Rain could talk some sense into him. Her dad wasn't going to like what he heard, but she was done for the day. Completely done.

Her dad could make his own choices.

She lifted the cell out of her pocket. It was time to think about what she was going to do with her life and stop worrying about the *talk* that would go on without her. "Call me if you need me."

Rain nodded. Her dad nodded. She nodded. Shit, she had to get out of here before she forgot everything she learned about herself today.

She left the cabin, marched across the parking lot, and escaped the madness in the cabin to go work inside the bar. She picked up her step, anxious to find out how Torque was doing.

She should've paid more attention to him yesterday after she found out he was okay and her father hadn't seriously wounded him. Her priorities were wrong and until now, she hadn't seen how unfair she was being to Torque. She owed him an apology.

After that, she honestly didn't know what she was going to do.

She honored her position as his woman and wanted him back, but asking him to put up with her dad was too much for even her to handle, and he was a blood relative. She wasn't even sure Torque would want her to stay in Pitnam now that Los Li wasn't after her and she had a somewhat normal life back in Cali to go home to now.

Bruce waylaid her at the end of the hallway. "Hey…how are you doing?"

"Fine." She bobbed her head side to side to let him know she'd been better. "How's Torque?"

"Haven't seen him." Bruce flipped the towel in his hand over his shoulder.

Her shoulders slumped. "But you've heard from him, right? Someone has checked in on him?"

"Yeah, I'm sure he's fine." Bruce backed away. "It's Torque. You can't kill the son of a bitch."

She snarled. "That's not funny."

"It sort of is...he's been shot four times now." Bruce grinned, and quickly turned serious. "He's all right, sweetheart. Torque wouldn't want you to worry about him. He got a couple scratches. I'm sure he'll be here when he can."

"You don't know that though," she muttered, pulling out the cell phone Rain gave her last night.

She clicked on Torque's already listed number and held the cell to her ear. After five rings, the phone disconnected instead of going to voice mail. Where was he?

Maybe he was feeling better and thought he'd go to the garage and work. She hurried into the bar after Bruce. "What's Shift's Garage's phone number?"

"He's not there," Bruce said, wiping down the counter. "And before you ask, I don't know where he is."

"Well, who would know?" she asked.

"No clue." He shrugged. "Delivery is in the back room if you're here to get started doing your job. Taylor needs you to check the boxes. She doesn't think they sent the right order."

"I'm skipping my first break and taking the extra time at lunch." She blew out her breath, and headed to the storage room.

Her lunch break wasn't for another four hours, which was after the dinner crowd left and before the evening drinkers came. She pushed through the door. Since she had an hour and fifteen minutes, it'd allow her enough time to run over to Torque's house and check on him if she couldn't get ahold of him by then. It wasn't like him not to check in with the club during the day, and that worried her.

Taylor stuck her head in the room. "Did you find the boxes?"

"Yeah." She held up the handful of menus. "These are the menus I ordered."

"Really?" Taylor leaned against the doorframe. "We're going to a smaller offering?"

She put the menus back. "Rain wants to maximize what works, and trim back on what doesn't. People come here for burgers, appetizers, and drinks. They can get steak and baked potatoes at the hotel lounge in town. Besides, saltier foods mean more drinks ordered to quench the customer's thirst. That's where the money comes from, and—"

"The more tips the waitresses get in their pocket." Taylor smiled. "I like it. You're good for Cactus Cove. I loved Gladys, but changes make the world go round."

"I'm trying," she said, following Taylor back into the bar.

Taylor nudged her arm. "By the way, thanks for the overtime. Every little bit helps."

She smiled, feeling good about helping Taylor and Slade. Her own life might be a mess, but she enjoyed her work and the friendships she'd made while at Cactus Cove. "Can I ask you something before you get back to work?"

"Sure." Taylor placed her arm on Brandy's wrist and led her over away from the counter. "What's up?"

"Has Slade seen Torque or talked to him today?" she asked.

Taylor looked away. "Don't ask me that question."

She rocked back a foot, pressing a hand to her mouth. "Oh, God."

"No, no, oh God, no." Taylor grabbed Brandy's arms. "He's hurting, but he's moving around. I think he's mainly sore, which is to be expected."

Her heart raced and she sucked in air. This didn't make sense. If he was up and doing okay, then why hadn't he rode over and seen her?

"Then where is he?" she asked.

Taylor shook her head. "I don't know. Honestly, I really don't. Slade talked to him early this morning and went over to his house for a couple hours. When I asked Slade later, he said it was club business. That's probably all it is. You know these guys, if it has to do with Bantorus, they don't tell the old ladies."

Old ladies. She bit down on the side of her cheek. Was she still his woman?

After walking away from him when he needed her last night to deal with her dad, she couldn't blame him if he hated her. "Okay, thanks. You better get to work, and I need to check in with Bruce."

For the next four hours, she kept herself busy to keep her mind off Torque, her dad with Rain smoking pot in her cabin, and concentrated on getting through the evening until lunchtime. The minute it turned eight o'clock, she skipped eating, ran out the back door to jump in her car to go to Torque's house, and came to a complete stop.

She peered around the lot. The spot where she'd last parked her car was empty.

Chapter Twenty Three

At almost midnight, Torque rolled into the parking lot of Cactus Cove. It'd taken him longer than he thought to finish today, and he knew by the many phone calls he made to Bruce that Brandy's patience had left after her mid-shift lunch break.

Torque parked his Harley and peeled off his shirt. The constant ache in his shoulder turned into sharp throbbing as the dried material broke away from his wound. He rotated his arm and looked over the slice the bullet made, which still oozed. The bullet gouged a nice sized indent into his muscle, and he hoped the antibiotics Ginger brought him this morning did the trick.

His leg was fine, more like road rash than anything, though the meaty part of his calf consisted of a bruise the color of his motorcycle. He should've taken a day off and recuperated, but he had no extra time to waste. Brandy was not going to push him away a minute longer.

He removed a clean T-shirt from his bag on the side of his bike and stuffed the dirty one away. After he redressed, he walked into the bar. He took a second to locate his woman, and when he found her over by the pool table, arms crossed, nodding as if she was listening to Pauline, he tensed. He knew the raised brows, the vacate stare, the plastered half smile she gave Orca's woman. Brandy was deep in her head, and that was the last place he wanted her to be.

When he'd had her alone, she was always right there with him, promising forever on the back of his bike. Until her dad came, and he'd seen Brandy revert to the woman who got in his face the first time he met her. The light went out of her eyes, and the happy out of her world.

Yet, he couldn't help admiring her for the love she had for her dad, and not letting the hurt of her childhood bring her down. She pulled on her thigh-high boots and kicked ass. His chest warmed. Hell, she'd kicked his ass and he fell like a rock for her.

How he'd come to the place in his life where he needed someone else more than he needed his freedom was beyond understanding. He loved her, and the kind of love he had for her went deeper than the blood flowing in his veins. She was life.

She gave him beauty where before he had darkness. He'd never heard a softer sound than her whispering to him right before she fell asleep or felt the touch of a woman who was content to hug him. She gave until she exhausted herself, and he wanted to give her everything until she lit up his world with sunshine.

He rubbed his hand over his jaw, because he looked like a damn fool thinking words he'd never spoken to anyone before in his life. He stepped toward her and her eyes swept across the room and landed on him. Her chest rose with her gasp and her eyes shone bright. He quickened his steps, and if he hadn't been watching, he would've missed that first honest reaction when he caught her unaware. All wasn't lost.

By the time he reached her, she hid everything from her. Though the rigidness of her body was a sure sign that she wasn't happy.

She lifted her chin. "Where's my car?"

He bent his head and said in her ear. "I got rid of it."

"Why?" She pursed her lips, and damn if he didn't want to kiss them until they were soft and greedy for more.

"It's a Los Li car, and I won't have it on Bantorus land," he said.

She studied his eyes, and her body softened. Then she looked at his shoulders and down at his jeans. "You're okay?"

He sucked in a breath. "I'm fine."

Her gaze settled back on his eyes and her spine stiffened again. "How will I get back to Cali if you sold my car?"

He glanced over to the others watching them, and said, "Come with me."

"I'm still working," she said, not giving him an inch.

"Not for long." He lifted his chin, sought out Bruce, motioned with his head toward the door, and got a nod back in answer. "Your shifts over, and I have something to show you."

"It better be a new car, because I don't have the money to buy another one," she said.

He took her hand and led her across the room, thankful she followed him because if she hadn't he would've picked her up and packed her over his shoulder, and bled all over the fucking floor. Outside, he went straight to his motorcycle and handed her a helmet.

"Hop on," he said.

"I can't." She stood in the parking lot and glanced in the direction of the cabin. "Rain's been with my dad all night and when I left them to go back to work after lunch, my dad was flying high on pot and I think Rain was enjoying watching my dad get stoned. My dad was actually…I hate to say it…but I think he was okay with staying in the cabin."

"I heard." He took the helmet from her and put it on her head. "We'll only be gone an hour tops. Give me your time."

She stepped toward his Harley and hesitated. "Where are you taking me?"

She wasn't going to make this easy, and he loved that about her. He kissed her hard, pulled back, and smiled. "Home, sunshine."

On the ride to his house, he took his time. Selfish and feeling better than he had all day, he wanted to slow down and enjoy having her pressed against his body. For once, he had something bigger planned than nailing her until they were both exhausted.

Besides, she was worn down and defensive, trying to keep a hold on everything she held dear to her. Everyone expected her to jump…him, her dad, Rain. She needed time to shelf her responsibilities for once and take the time for herself that she deserved.

He had plans for her that'd make sure she never had to take on too much again.

He wanted to put his mark on her, give his life and live the remaining days doing the things he'd never given himself time to dream about, and he wanted to do all those things with her. Brandy brought that out of him.

Before her, he might've been out of prison, but he'd created his own walls to protect himself from allowing other to hurt him. Not any longer, because everything would change today.

The porch light lit up the driveway. He pulled clear up to the garage door and parked the Harley. Brandy climbed off the bike first, and he followed. She stood beside him and took off her helmet, setting it on the bike. He let her have time to notice the changes.

The manicured lawn Jedman spent the day cutting, the flowers Tori and Crystal planted early this morning in the new flowerbed that he couldn't give a shit about, but the Bantorus women swore Brandy would love. He stood back and let her walk out into the grass a few feet. Her head tilted one way before going the other, and she had yet to say a word.

Her hair blew in the cool night air. He had a hard time believing she was here. He hooked his hands in his pockets and breathed in. She belonged here more than he did because without her, he'd never be happy.

Brandy walked the sidewalk to the front door and peered up at the chrome glass fixture surrounding six bulbs, shielding her eyes against the brightness. He joined her and opened the new screen door. She walked past him, looking at him with questions in her eyes, but had yet to voice what she was thinking. He had no idea what was going through her head.

He flipped the light switch on inside the house and entered the living room. The Bantorus women had tried to talk him into decorating the inside as well as the outside, but he wanted Brandy to pick out colors, pillows, and all those things women like to do herself.

Slipping his hand into hers, he walked her down the hallway, past his bedroom, and opened the spare room. He'd left the light on, and the new bed with the black and red comforter and six-drawer dresser almost appeared too big for the room. It wasn't much, but there was a private entrance with the sliding door on the back wall.

Brandy stepped inside and ran her fingers over the poster of Muhammad Ali holding the championship belt. She sniffed, and he leaned against the wall and put his hands in his pockets. He wanted to say so many things, but he'd never give his feelings for her justice.

She set the boxing gloves hanging on the bedpost to swinging, and laughed softly. "You know, he'll use these against you. He'll pick an argument, cuff you on the shoulder, and he'll have you out in the yard and using them on you before I can stop him."

"Maybe he can teach me a thing or two," he said.

She glanced at him and continued studying the room. "Rain told me he offered dad a job managing the bar this afternoon. Dad seemed happy about the offer. Though, I wonder…if the joint he was smoking had anything to do with his compliance."

He nodded, even though her back was to him. Rain letting Torque take responsibility for Haas cost him the price of sitting out on three runs, and clean up if Brandy's dad started a fight in the bar.

"It was you who did that for me," she stated, turning around, not even questioning his motives.

He shrugged. "Man needs a purpose. He needs to see his daughter content. I want to be the man who gives his daughter her happy back."

"Torque, I—"

"I'm not finished talking." He pushed off the wall, feeling old and beat, and approached her. "You and me have seen hell and survived. Never thought I'd reach out for someone offering me the sweetness in life, but here I am. I'm not going to let you walk away from me. You've made it possible to recognize what I've never given myself a chance at dreaming about, and I'm selfish, stubborn—"

"An asshole," she whispered in that soft voice that grabbed him by the throat and refused to let go.

He cupped her face, swiping the tear that escaped with his thumb. "Yeah, an asshole that won't let the best thing he's ever had slip away to California."

"Babe," she whispered, her voice cracking.

"Not letting go of you, sunshine. I will fucking flip your life around and give you everything you need and want. Your dad can live with us, right here in this room. He can work at the bar alongside you, and you'll have the security of doing what you love while knowing your dad is okay. Then at night, you're in my bed or on my couch or sitting out on my porch with me, giving me sunshine in a dark life. In the morning, I want to start my day between your legs with your arms around me, feeling your happy. If making you happy means staying up all night listening to you talk, I will. I'll let you make me respectable in the neighborhood, if that's your thing. But, I want you for the rest of my life."

"Why?" she mouthed.

He laid his forehead on hers. "Because I love you, sunshine."

"You do?" She laid her hands on his chest.

He nodded. "Claimed you, put you on the back of my Harley, didn't I? There was never a possibility that I'd let you go."

"I've been so wrong, worrying about my dad. I should've gone with you last night. I couldn't see what I was doing to you or me. I'm even holding my dad back from being content, because I'm scared of losing another person in my life. Until last night when you weren't with me, I thought I knew what I was doing, but I found out what I really need. You." She kissed his lips, his cheeks, his neck, and in between kisses she said, "I love you. And, that love no longer scares me, because you more than fill my life, you *are* life, babe."

That was all he needed to hear in that impossible sexy voice of hers. He lowered his head, took her mouth, and kissed her with the promise never to take that love for granted.

She brought her hands up to his neck and kissed him back, opening herself so that he could fill her and give her everything she needed. He didn't disappoint.

He delved his tongue into her mouth, connecting with her soul. On stroke, taste, and he went back for more. The pleasurable dance healed his tired body. Hard and possessive of his women, he pulled back an inch. "You're gonna have to help me, sunshine."

"How?" She peered up at him with arousal shining brightly in her eyes.

"I need you, and I don't think I can throw you on the bed tonight. So you're going to have to take my hand and let me walk you there," he said.

"I can do better than that, babe." She caught her lip between her teeth, shifted to his side, and put her arm around him.

One aching step at a time, he made it across the hallway and to their bed. He managed to strip out of his clothes while keeping his gaze on her, loving the way she hurried and stood before him without any misgivings.

She reached for him, but pulled her hands back before they could touch his upper body. "God, babe…your shoulder."

Angry red and sore, his shoulder would heal in time. He walked her backward, laid her on the bed, and stood there admiring his woman. "It's fine. I'm fine."

The way her hips flared beneath a slim waist, the high breasts— more than she needed, were perfect for him and drove him crazy. He opened the condom he'd taken out of his wallet, and rolled it on his hardness. Unashamed, she spread her legs. He was a damn lucky man.

He went down on one arm. Brandy sprawled her hands on his abdomen, and guided him onto his back. He let out his breath in relief. Brandy straddled his legs and smiled down on him. He slid his hand between their bodies, and found her wet and ready.

"Mouth on me," he said.

She lowered her head and kissed him. His balls tightened at the way the weight of her breasts brushed his chest, her hips moving on his hand, and her tongue dancing with his. In this position, he connected with her fully.

Legs to legs. Chest to chest. Mouth to mouth. Linked together.

Brandy's body undulated atop him. Her sex ground down on his hand. She lifted her head, and there it was. That look, that softness, that whisper on his skin, settled him. Yet, behind the look, there was the openness he'd needed, and she gave him freely. He could see what she was thinking.

He was in her head, and she was happy.

"Go ahead, sunshine." He removed his hand and dropped his arm to the mattress. "Make us both happy."

That's when his woman braced herself on his abdomen, slid her sweet pussy over his cock, and she gave him more than he ever dreamed. Sliding, grinding, squeezing, she set a rhythm that took him to the top and kept him vibrating. With each movement, she rubbed her sex on him and he loved every second. His toes curled and he couldn't take any more.

"I got you," he said on a grunt, grasping her hips and helping her continue her pleasurable assault.

His balls drew up, straining for relief. He groaned, and could feel her insides tightening, pulsing, sucking around him as she climaxed. "So fucking gorgeous."

She sank down on him, bowed her head, and her hair swept his chest. He flew. Every inch of his body screamed and he unloaded the very essence of him inside of her. He hooked her neck, bringing her down, and laying her on his chest.

In slow circular motion, he rubbed her warm, bare back with his good arm, while catching his breath. Full weight on him, she laid loose limbed and exhausted. He wasn't in any better shape. There wasn't a working muscle in his body.

"Love you, sunshine," he whispered against her hair.

She lifted her head and whispered back, "Love you, babe."

Just like that, she gave him everything he needed.

She sighed in contentment. "I can't believe you gave me flowers in the yard…a yard that's mowed."

He captured her face. "I'd do anything for you."

And, there would be more beautiful things in her life. This was just the beginning. The more he experienced her happy, the more he wanted to grasp everything there was to make his woman's life perfect.

Chapter Twenty Four

Six Months Later—

Three hours earlier, Cactus Cove closed to the public, and every Bantorus member filled the bar. Brandy slid a tray of empty beer mugs into the bin, and then worked her way through the crowd. The atmosphere had only grown louder as the night went on.

Three months ago, Rain had added new entertainment onto the Bantorus roster and the members loved to come in late Sunday and watch. She walked to Torque and slid her arm around his waist.

He looked down at her and grinned. "All done?"

"Yep." She placed her hand on his stomach. "How's he doing?"

Torque motioned his head. "See for yourself?"

Her dad stood in the middle of the cleared area in the bar, atop the rolled out mat. In front of him, Kurt, Slade's son, stood getting his hands wrapped with tape. The boy gazed up at her dad as he listened intently to her father's instructions. A few feet away, the prospect, Tim, bounced on his bare feet, loosening up.

"Kurt's so young. It's not fair to pit him against Tim. He's five years older and thirty pounds heavier than Kurt." She glanced at her dad.

In ratty old sweat pants and a muscle shirt, her dad hooked Kurt's neck and brought him close. She smiled, because not only had her dad fallen right into helping orchestrate the workings of the bar, he'd jumped at Rain's offer to start a boxing club for the younger members and prospects.

Slade walked up to his son, massaged Kurt's shoulders while he talked to him. Brandy loved watching the two of them together. She knew exactly what Kurt would look like when he grew up a few more inches and aged a few more years. Taylor's concern over the amount of girls dropping by the house was real. Kurt had that badboy quiet presence that fascinated every female.

Kurt showed a real talent for keeping his head and outlasting the older boys in the makeshift ring the last couple of Sundays. She hoped this time he wasn't over his head, and her dad wasn't the one pushing him to go up against someone older and bigger.

"Let 'em fight, amigo," Raul yelled over the crowd, lifting a twenty dollar bill in one hand, while slinging his other arm around Crystal.

Raul wasn't letting Crystal get too far from his side lately. She laid her head against Torque. Tori informed them that Crystal had her tongue pierced a few days ago, and since Brandy hadn't heard her friend talk in two days, she suspected the rumors were true. Although, she'd caught Raul and Crystal kissing many times before disappearing from the bar. Whatever was happening between them, they had it going on.

Gladys climbed onto the mat, and her dad held out his hand to steady her on the unstable ground. Brandy leaned away from

Torque to keep them in sight and then stared in surprise. Her dad spoke low to Gladys and smiled at her afterward. Smiled.

"Uh, babe..." She tilted her head and kept watching the ring. "What's going on with my dad and Gladys?"

Torque leaned toward her, getting a better look through the crowd. "Nothing. Why?"

"Look at them." She gazed up at Torque. "He's talking and I saw a smile."

"Don't know," he mumbled, putting his mug to his lips and drinking. "I heard Gladys cooked him dinner the other night though."

"What?" She leaned closer. "Are you kidding?"

He shook his head. "Nope."

This was unbelievable. She stared at her dad. He'd never paid any woman any attention since her mom died. She raked her teeth over her bottom lip and it hit her. Her dad was doing better than she'd ever seen him. He deserved the same thing she'd found since arriving in Pitnam, and she hoped that whatever developed between him and Gladys was good for him.

Jedman came up to Torque and spoke privately with him. Torque nodded and watched him walk away. She waited a few seconds, and when Torque didn't volunteer any information about what was going on, she asked, "Everything okay?"

He shrugged. "Word just came through Lagsturns MC that Radiant was murdered."

She covered her throat with her hand. "Then it's over, and you don't have anything to worry about with Los Li, right?"

"It's over," he mumbled, holding her a little bit tighter.

The news should've relieved her, but there was always someone to step up and take Radiant's place. She swallowed hard, and pushed the information away. Tonight wasn't about the dangers of belonging to a Bantorus MC member and the chaos that came with them. Tonight was about relaxing, being around family, and going forward.

Brandy spotted Tori making her way toward her. Without letting go of Torque, she snagged Tori's hand when she drew close.

"Babysitter tonight?" she asked.

Tori laughed. "Yes, and in typical Rain fashion, he brought me here on a date because he wants to support his *boys*."

"Aw…we're going to have to talk some sense into that man," she laughed.

"He promised me a ride around town before we go home to relieve the babysitter, so I'm holding him to it." Tori grinned. "There's a sweet, private spot along the river that we'll probably stop at too."

"Gotcha." Brandy laughed. "So, who's Rain betting on?

Tori leaned closer. "Kurt. That boy can't do anything wrong in his eyes."

"Good choice." She squeezed Tori's hand. "Why don't you come by the house next week? I want to show you what I bought for Slade and Taylor's housewarming present. I'm not sure if it goes with her kitchen colors or not."

"That sounds fun. I'll bring coffee and Lilly with me." Tori kissed her cheek. "I'm going to go find Rain and work my magic to see if we can slip out of here early."

Her dad bellowed the opening announcement, rattling off the stats of both boxers. She hugged Torque's side; feeling at home and more content than ever—which was a surprise, because she was happy falling more in love with Torque every day.

An even bigger surprise came last weekend when her dad announced he was moving into Brandy's old cabin behind the bar. Everything was working out better than expected. Her dad enjoyed coaching and training the boys during his free time away from the bar, and now there was Gladys appearing in her dad's life.

A bubble of amusement and hope left her smiling. Suddenly, she wanted to get out of her. She went up on her tiptoes and leaned on Torque. "Let's go home, babe."

His brows lifted and he focused on her mouth. "You don't want to watch the fight?"

She smiled and shook her head. That's all it took, and he grasped her hand and led her out of the bar. Outside, she laughed and spun around to walk backward in front of him. One thing that hadn't changed was Torque's willingness to spend time with her whenever she needed him.

"Before I take you home and sink myself between your legs, how about we go for a ride?" Torque grabbed her hips and brought her to a stop.

"Can I touch you while we ride?" She grinned, running her finger along his lower lip.

"Yeah." He snapped his teeth and caught her finger in his mouth.

Her laughter ended on a squeak. "Make it a fast ride home, babe," she whispered.

His eyes flared in that special way they often did when she talked. He let go of her finger, and she kissed his lips softly. "Really fast."

"Right." He swooped her up in his arms and headed straight toward his Harley. "Let's roll."

On the back of his motorcycle, she wrapped her arms around his waist, laid her front against the back of his leather vest, and hugged her man. He roared out of the parking lot. She closed her eyes and smiled. Sometimes the happiness overwhelmed her, and all she could do was hold on and enjoy the ride.

The End

Author Bio

Top Selling Romance Author, Debra Kayn, lives with her family at the foot of the Bitterroot Mountains in beautiful Idaho. She enjoys riding motorcycles, playing tennis, fishing, and driving the men crazy in the garage.

Her love of family ties and laughter makes her a natural to write heartwarming contemporary stories to the delight of her readers. Oh, let's cut to the chase. She loves to write about *REAL MEN* and the *WOMEN* who love them.

When Debra was nineteen years old, a man kissed her without introducing himself. When they finally came up for air, the first words out of his mouth were…will you have my babies? Considering Debra's weakness for a sexy, badass man, who is strong enough to survive her attitude, she said yes. A quick wedding at the House of Amour and four babies later, she's living her own romance book.

Website: www.debrakayn.com
Twitter: www.twitter.com/DebraKayn
Facebook: www.facebook.com/DebraKaynFanPage

Debra Kayn's Backlist

Breathing His Air – Bantorus Motorcycle Club
Aching To Exhale – Lagsturns Motorcycle Club
Soothing His Madness – Bantorus Motorcycle Club
Grasping for Freedom – Bantorus Motorcycle Club
Fighting To Ride – Bantorus Motorcycle Club
Laying Down His Colors – Bantorus Motorcycle Club, anthology titled Melt My Heart
Archer, A Hard Body Novel, book 1
Weston, A Hard Body Novel, book 2
Biker Babe in Black, The Chromes and Wheels Gang, book 1
Ride Free, The Chromes and Wheels Gang, book 2
Healing Trace
Wildly, Playing For Hearts, book 1
Seductively, Playing For Hearts, book 2
Conveniently, Playing For Hearts, book 3
Secretly, Playing For Hearts, book 4
Surprisingly, Playing For Hearts, book 5
Chantilly's Cowboy, The Sisters of McDougal Ranch, book 1
Val's Rancher, The Sisters of McDougal Ranch, book 2
Margot's Lawman, The Sisters of McDougal Ranch, book 3
Florentine's Hero, The Sisters of McDougal Ranch, book 4
Suite Cowboy
Hijinks
Resurrecting Charlie's Girl
Betraying the Prince
Love Rescued Me
Double Agent
Breaking Fire Code

Sneak Peek at Chapter One – **Aching To Exhale**

Chapter One

Close to twenty motorcycles, parked in one perfect line, took up the sidewalk outside High and Dry Lounge. Crystal Rose hesitated for a heartbeat before continuing to walk through the parking lot. The eleven months since losing Raul Sanchez and the Lagsturns Motorcycle Club had reduced her to paranoia.

Every biker driving by left her weak. Men of Latino descent caused her to take a second look, half hoping it was Raul, and panic at the thought it could be him.

It was never him.

Crystal hurried through the double doors into work. She'd stayed too long in one place for her comfort. That had to be the reason why her legs shook and her nerves were raw and on edge. She hefted her bag over her shoulder. In two more weeks, she'd have enough money to move on.

"Crystal, you're late." Dean, her boss, hurried out from behind the bar and pushed her through the lounge toward the back dressing room.

"I'm twenty minutes early." She glanced behind her as she walked. "I took the number three bus to make sure I arrived before my first set."

"I switched your schedule with Ella. Her kid's sick and she's not going to make it in to open the show. I would've called, but you haven't left a phone number in the office." Dean planted his hand on her back and catapulted her through the swinging door to the dressing room. "You've got five minutes to get on stage and make the men happy."

"Shit," she mumbled, throwing her bag down.

She stripped out of her old baggy Jimmy Hendrix T-shirt and black yoga pants she'd bought at Goodwill when she'd arrived in Palm Springs. Staying in the rough part of town forced her to take precautions with her appearance. She dumbed down her style to make sure no one followed her to the job or back to the motel after work. Dancing for money was a filthy job, but she was good at what she did.

In a desperate need to hide against the reality of her life, she stood in front of the mirror, applied heavy black eyeliner, and sprayed her hair out so far from her head Whitesnake would hire her over Tawny Kitaen for their next video. Then she dressed in her skimpy two-piece, deep purple colored bikini she'd altered with silver sequins and black tassels.

Five minutes later, she sauntered out onto the unlit stage. She looked below the dim lounge lights at the men crowding the stage, and raised her gaze to the darkened shadows standing in the back. Everything appeared normal, if not a bit quieter than usual for a Saturday night.

Grabbing the pole, she waited for the lights operator to put the spotlight on her. Prepared for the onslaught of blindness, she swung into her routine with practiced ease. Her show was simple, really.

She pretended she was alone. The pole was Raul. He'd often stand in the middle of the room at the club and let her dance circles around him. Too tough, too smooth, too guarded to let himself have fun in front of the other bikers, but there was always something about the way he watched her when she danced for him that told her he enjoyed what she was doing.

She could almost feel the soft denim of his worn jeans in her mind. She hooked her calf around the pole. The warmth of his body, rock solid, standing there, soaking her all in. She let her head fall back as her hair swept the floor. How many times had he whispered *'mi vida'* with his silver tongue, knowing it made her wet for him?

Her circular momentum stopped and she straddled the pole. She reached above her and pulled herself against the apparatus. Hand over hand, the pole warmed to the touch by the lights shining on her gave the illusion it was alive. Raul always put up with a lot from her, but the moment she finished dancing, he'd hook her neck and pull her in for a kiss.

God, the man could kiss. He made love with his tongue, caressing her soul, and she was powerless to deny him anything he wanted. She turned and leaned her back against her prop, reached above her, and slid into a squat.

The music quickened, and she grasped the pole with both hands, took two running steps, and held herself horizontal to the floor as she descended. Around and around, until her foot skimmed the floor and the lights went out. She lay there, dizzy.

She should've eaten today.

She pushed herself off the floor and straightened. Three steps toward the back of the stage, she ran into a solid wall. She braced her hands against the barrier and clutched leather. She inhaled. Sweet mint and leather with a hint of tobacco curled her toes.

Adrenaline flooded her veins, fear stole her breath, and despite her fight or flight response, her fingers sprawled against his chest, grabbing as much of him as she could before she escaped. She pushed. "Let me go."

"Not this time. Scream or fight me and every man in here will wish he hadn't come tonight." Raul slipped her hand into his, holding her solidly in place and led her off the stage.

She tugged on her arm to get away, but he never budged and he wasn't letting go. A scream built in her chest, but stayed locked inside of her. For how much she feared being in the hands of the Lagsturns MC again, she couldn't make herself bring trouble down on Raul's head.

Outside in the parking lot, she jerked her hand out of his grasp and faced him under the glow of the streetlight. The only man who could cause her heart to stop beating stood in front of her, his eyes blacker than death. Her chest tightened, making her ache to exhale. Raul Sanchez's appearance back into her life meant trouble wasn't far behind.

Confident, on the verge of cocky, Raul rocked back on the heels of his biker boots, slipped his fingers into the pockets of his faded black Levi's and gazed at her intently, waiting her out. She dropped her gaze to his chest. A white T-shirt with the arms cut off to fit his muscular frame—he hated the tightness across his shoulders—and the Lagsturns' cut proved she wasn't dreaming. She swallowed in distress, but the way her stomach tightened at seeing him called her a liar for being afraid.

His Latino charm and drop dead sexy good looks made her a devote believer in what could only be described as her cult-ish love for him. Her breath hitched in her chest and her tongue stuck to the roof of her mouth.

She soaked in the man who'd owned her for nine months, treated her better than he did his Harley Davidson, showed her the world from his eyes, and set her body on fire—in the best possible way.

Then he'd changed.

"Are you done?" He lifted his brow.

She straightened her back and crossed her arms, suddenly aware she only had on three triangles of purple material and sequins, and he'd caught her ogling him. "I have two more shows."

"That's not what I'm talking about and you know it." He stepped forward and lowered his voice. "I can make you come with me or you can relive old times and climb onto the back of my bike, plaster yourself against my body, and love doing it."

She shivered remembering how much she enjoyed riding with him and going by the upward curl of his lip, he knew what she was thinking. She planted both of her hands on his chest and shoved. "I'm not going anywhere with you. I need to work."

Instead of letting her leave, he dipped and grabbed her around her thighs, throwing her over his shoulders. Disoriented and upside down, she grabbed on to the back of his jeans and kicked her feet. "Damn you, put me down."

He slapped her ass. She screamed, hating the way the desire to escape him fled. Each step away from the lounge marked by an exhale pushed out of her body as she bounced on his shoulder.

Raul stopped and heaved her off his shoulder and into his arms, letting her slowly slide along his rock hard body until she stood on solid ground again. She held on to him as the world righted itself and she was no longer dizzy.

Her reflection shone in his dark obsidian colored eyes. She looked away out of guilt.

In the past, she'd begged, bargained, used, lied to earn her way back into Raul's good graces, and failed miserably. In her desperation to save their relationship, she'd made a fool of herself and found herself escorted onto a bus heading out of town and fearing for her life.

That fear kept her from returning to Southern Oregon, home to the Lagsturns Motorcycle Club. Back to the one man she loved.

Not that she regretted her time with him, never that. She'd go back in a heartbeat if it was safe to stay with him. It was the guilt of keeping secrets from Raul that she regretted. She wasn't good enough for a man like Raul Sanchez, and she'd never be able to tell him what forced her into hiding from the world.

Raul hooked her neck, bringing her attention back to him. "I'm going to get on my bike, and you're going to climb on behind me."

That's when the truth hit her upside the head. Whatever Raul asked her to do, she'd do her best to make sure she made him happy. Because in her heart, she could never tell him no…and that was part of their problem.

She swallowed hard, glancing down the line of riders waiting for her to follow their president's orders. God, she missed them. "Fine. Let me get my clothes and bag first."

He walked over to his bike, opened his saddlebag, and tossed her a pair of jeans and his leather coat. "There's no time. We need to roll."

She shoved her legs in his jeans and held the waist. He helped her on the back of his bike. Before she could question him, he sped off into the night. She wrapped her arms around his waist and closed her eyes. For now, she'd take what she could from him. When he calmed down and allowed her to talk, she'd ask him to let her go, for both their sakes.

Made in the USA
Lexington, KY
11 October 2015